She Felt Like Running Late At The Ball.

If she stayed until morning, she was likely to turn back into a charwoman. But if she left now, Ethan would continue to believe she'd been a beautiful— if temporary—princess.

Her heart squeezed at the thought of never seeing him again, but she didn't have a choice. It was better to go now.

Before he found out who she really was, and began to hate her for lying to him.

She was halfway into the hall, but couldn't bring herself to leave. Not just yet.

Tiptoeing back to the bed, she leaned over Ethan's still form.

"Goodbye," she whispered, tears springing to her eyes.

He never moved, never gave any sign that she'd woken him. And that was for the best, she knew.

She hurried from the room and out of the apartment...just like Cinderella running from her Prince Charming.

Dear Reader,

Sit back, relax and indulge yourself with all the fabulous offerings from Silhouette Desire this October. Roxanne St. Claire is penning the latest DYNASTIES: THE ASHTONS with *The Highest Bidder.* Youngest Ashton sibling, Paige, finds herself participating in a bachelorette auction and being "won" by a sexy stranger. Strangers also make great protectors, as demonstrated by Annette Broadrick in *Danger Becomes You,* her most recent CRENSHAWS OF TEXAS title.

Speaking of protectors, Michelle Celmer's heroine in *Round-the-Clock Temptation* gets a bodyguard of her very own: a member of the TEXAS CATTLEMAN'S CLUB. Linda Conrad wraps up her miniseries THE GYPSY INHERITANCE with *A Scandalous Melody.* Will this mysterious music box bring together two lonely hearts? For something a little darker, why not try *Secret Nights at Nine Oaks* by Amy J. Fetzer? A handsome recluse, an antebellum mansion—two great reasons to stay indoors. And be sure to catch Heidi Betts's *When the Lights Go Down,* the story of a plain-Jane librarian out to make some serious changes in her humdrum love life.

As you can see, Silhouette Desire has lots of great stories for you to enjoy. So spend this first month of autumn cuddled up with a good book—and come back next month for even more fabulous reads.

Enjoy!

Melissa Jeglinski

Melissa Jeglinski
Senior Editor
Silhouette Desire

Please address questions and book requests to:
Silhouette Reader Service
U.S.: 3010 Walden Ave., P.O. Box 1325, Buffalo, NY 14269
Canadian: P.O. Box 609, Fort Erie, Ont. L2A 5X3

WHEN THE LIGHTS GO DOWN

Heidi Betts

Published by Silhouette Books
America's Publisher of Contemporary Romance

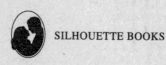

SILHOUETTE BOOKS

ISBN 0-373-76686-6

WHEN THE LIGHTS GO DOWN

Visit Silhouette Books at www.eHarlequin.com

Printed in U.S.A.

HEIDI BETTS

An avid romance reader since junior high school, Heidi knew early on that she wanted to write these wonderful stories of love and adventure. It wasn't until her freshman year of college, however, when she spent the entire night reading a romance novel instead of studying for finals, that she decided to take the road less traveled and follow her dream. In addition to reading, writing and romance, she is the founder of her local Romance Writers of America chapter and has a tendency to take injured and homeless animals of every species into her central Pennsylvania home.

Heidi loves to hear from readers. You can write to her at P.O. Box 99, Kylertown, PA 16847 (a SASE is appreciated but not necessary) or e-mail heidi@heidibetts.com. And be sure to visit www.heidibetts.com for news and information about upcoming books.

To my local RWA Chapter, Clearfield Area Romance Authors #167 (aka CARA)—Thank you for your dedication and friendship, and for making CARA such a success! Especially Cindy Musser and Joanne Emrick, who are always there when I need them, holding my hand and urging me on. I wish you all the very best with your own writing and will be standing there to cheer you every step of the way.

And always, for Daddy.

ACKNOWLEDGMENTS
With extra thanks, once again, to Sandy Rangel, who helped me with even more Georgetown details for this story—at the eleventh hour, no less. Any mistakes or inaccurate descriptions (intentional or otherwise) are entirely my own.

One

The moment Gwen Thomas opened her eyes, she knew it wasn't going to be a typical Friday in September. Oh, sure, she'd get up, get dressed and go to work just like any other day, but… She stared at the ceiling above her bed, trying to figure out why she felt so strange, almost depressed.

Then she remembered. It was her birthday. And not just any birthday—her thirty-first.

With a groan, she threw back the sheets and stomped to the bathroom. Thirty-one years old, but she felt more like fifty. Where had the time gone? And when had she turned into little more than a hamster on a wheel ... every day the same as the last, the scenery never changing?

Twenty-nine had come and gone. She'd barely noticed thirty, surviving that milestone with no hint at all of an early midlife crisis. But thirty-one.... She'd been upset about turning thirty-one for weeks.

Now her birthday had arrived and she was officially a thirty-one-year-old virgin.

An old maid.

Oh, God. The only thing missing was a houseful of cats. Thankfully, her apartment building didn't allow pets or she'd probably fit that part of the stereotype, too. Then again, she did have a lot of ceramic kitties scattered around the apartment.

How did a semi-attractive woman get to be thirty—let alone thirty-one—without ever going to bed with a man? Gwen wondered. She squeezed a dollop of paste onto her toothbrush and began to scrub.

Granted, her parents had been overly protective of her as a child, and she'd been shy and a bit of a bookworm in high school. But she'd dated some very nice guys in college. None of them had ever made her knees go weak or sent her heart beating out of control, though, which she supposed was why she'd never returned their advances.

After rinsing her mouth, she washed and dried her face, then lifted her head to glance in the mirror over the sink. She wasn't beautiful by any means, but she also didn't think her looks would send men running in fear.

Her eyes were a nice comforting brown, a few shades darker than her somewhat lackluster mouse-brown hair. And her figure was okay, if a bit small in all areas. She was petite, with breasts that would probably only fill a teacup if they were lucky. But still, it wasn't as if she had a hump or missing teeth.

Walking back into the bedroom, she stopped in front of her open closet and studied the lineup of dresses inside. For the first time she noticed how similar her entire wardrobe was. Some long, some short, but all sun- or baby-doll dresses in lightweight, floral fabrics. Lord, could she be any more *Little House on the Prairie?*

After closing the closet door, she plopped down at the foot of the bed and sighed with disgust. Thirty-one years old and she was still dressing the same as she had in high school. And she knew without having to pull them out that every pair of shoes she owned were flat and matronly, in one of two shades—black or brown. She still sported the same long, straight hair that reached the middle of her back and bangs cut across her forehead with almost military precision.

It was enough to make a girl curl up under the covers and never leave her apartment again.

The thought rattled Gwen. She refused to let another year come and go without at least attempting to take a bite out of life.

Rolling across the mattress, she picked up the phone and dialed the Georgetown branch of the D.C. Public Library by memory. When the head librarian and her boss, Marilyn Williams, answered, Gwen feigned a hoarse cough and asked for the day off.

Marilyn was suitably shocked by the request, considering Gwen had never asked to take a sick day before, but she quickly agreed and promised to call one of the part-time librarians to cover for Gwen if things got hectic.

As soon as she hung up, Gwen stripped out of her mint-green nightshirt—also covered in a tiny flowered pattern—and changed into one of her sadly out-of-date cotton tunics and a pair of shoes. She grabbed the phone book and began searching for a beauty shop, a nail salon and a trendy boutique, to start.

She wasn't sure yet exactly what she planned to do, but with any luck, this might just be the last day she was a thirty-one-year-old virgin.

Some nights, Ethan Banks stayed in his office high above the dance floor, feeling the rhythm of the loud music vibrate through the structure's steel beams while he worked at his desk or watched the flashy club-goers through the soundproof windows having the time of their lives. Other times, like tonight, he went downstairs and lent a hand behind the bar to mingle with the crowd.

The Hot Spot was one of downtown Georgetown's premiere nightclubs—and his pride and joy. He'd rented and completely renovated the rundown building nearly five years ago, and the place had been packed just about every night since.

He was proud of the club's success, but even prouder that he'd done it on his own, without a dime of his parents' money. Not that they hadn't offered. Jack and Karen Banks loved their children and supported all three in whatever they wanted to do with their lives. But Ethan hadn't wanted his family's wealth to have any impact on his personal successes or failures.

Of course, his decision to strike out on his own and actually work for something he wanted hadn't sat well with Susan. Which was why she was now his *ex*-wife.

Divorce hadn't been on his agenda, but being single certainly did have its perks. Especially for a man who owned the city's most popular nightclub.

A shapely blonde wearing rhinestone chandelier earrings and a hot-pink, skintight bodysuit unzipped nearly to her belly button rested her ample breasts on the bar and bounced in time with the blaring hip-hop tune while he mixed her a Screaming Orgasm. The way she was eyeing him, Ethan suspected that, if he wanted, he had a pretty good chance of taking her home after closing and giving her a taste of the real thing.

Thanks to The Hot Spot—and, he liked to think, his own charming personality—his bed was empty only when he wanted it to be.

He handed the blonde her drink and was about to lean forward to make his first move when a flash of gold at the end of the bar caught his attention. Cocking his head, he took in the olive green polyester jacket, slicked-back hair, and excessive jewelry of one of the club's regulars. An obvious sleazeball, the man made a habit of haunting The Hot Spot, hitting on everything that moved—everything female, at any rate.

Normally, Ethan considered him harmless. Or at least assumed that any woman dumb enough to hook up with the gigolo deserved what she got. But his eyes shifted to the man's current companion and something about her demeanor struck him as a little less worldly than the club's usual clientele.

She looked the part, in a little black dress, her auburn hair teased and sprayed. But he hadn't seen her dancing, she wasn't mingling with the crowd, and she didn't seem overly interested in whatever this throwback from the disco era was whispering in her ear. She simply stared down at the appletini she was stirring with a plastic swizzle stick, seemingly mesmerized by the liquid swirling round and round in the funnel-shaped glass.

He watched the guy run the backs of his fingers down the length of her bare arm. The auburn-haired woman lifted her head, turned to look at the man who was touching her and blinked as though she'd just woken from a particularly confusing dream.

Silver teardrops dangled from her earlobes, reflecting the strobe lights circling the dance floor at her back. Her gaze lowered to the dark fingertips resting against her pale white skin before she licked her lips, swallowed, then slowly nodded her head.

The slick-haired fellow hopped off his high bar chair as if his pants were on fire. The woman finished the rest of her drink, wrapped her hand around the small, beaded purse beside her glass and followed suit. A sick feeling slid through Ethan's gut.

Something didn't feel right about what he was witnessing. He didn't normally get involved in his customers' affairs, but when he looked at the auburn-haired woman and the polyester-clad man, all he could picture was a big, ugly spider lying in wait for a tiny, innocent butterfly to unwittingly land in its web.

Busty blonde suddenly forgotten, Ethan walked to the end of the bar, stopping only long enough to tell his regular bartender that he was once again on his own.

Rounding the bar, Ethan stepped in front of the gigolo before he could drag the woman off to God knew where. The man raised his eyes to Ethan's, a smirk twisting the pencil-thin mustache above his upper lip.

Ethan gave the guy a once-over, decided not to waste his time, then turned his attention to the petite woman standing none too steadily at his side.

"Hello there," he said, offering his hand. "I'm Ethan Banks, owner of The Hot Spot."

Her gaze never shifted from his as she took his hand. Not counting her stiletto heels and her teased hair, the top of her head would probably only reach the underside of his chin. Since he was exactly six feet tall, he figured that put her somewhere around five foot three or four inches.

He usually gravitated toward tall, leggy women who could take care of themselves—the polar opposite of this waiflike creature. Maybe that was why he felt this sudden urge to protect her from predators like her current companion.

Leaning forward, he pressed his mouth to her ear and raised his voice to be heard over the pounding music. "I don't mean to intrude, but it looks like you've had a bit too much to drink, and I think you might want to reconsider your decision to leave with this stranger. As owner, I assure you that I will see you home safely."

She nodded and leaned heavily against his side.

"Sorry, buddy," he told the man, who had turned a mottled red with indignation. "Looks like I'll be taking over from here."

Without waiting for a response, Ethan wrapped an arm around the young woman's waist and guided her through the crowd to the club's entrance. Once outside he led her to the edge of the sidewalk and scanned traffic for an available taxi.

"So what's your name?" he asked.

Gwen blinked, waiting for her eyes to adjust from the darkness of the club to the brightness cast by the streetlight over their heads. She still wasn't sure what had driven her to leave with one complete stranger over another. The only thing she could think was that the first man who'd approached her at the bar had been a little creepy and not terribly attractive, while the man who now held her hand was very attractive and made tiny fireworks go off low in her belly.

He had dark, almost black hair that was long on the sides but shorter in the back. His eyes appeared hazel, but could have been green, and his sapphire-blue jacket was tailored to fit the line of his strong, broad shoulders. He was tall, too. So tall that she had to tip her head to look at him, even in her heels.

Raking the length of his exceedingly masculine body, she finally caught his eye and recalled that he'd asked for her name.

She cleared her throat in embarrassment. "Gwen," she answered. "Gwen Thomas."

"Gwen." A small smile touched his lips, sending

another explosion skyrocketing through her system. "That's a pretty name. So tell me, Gwen Thomas, have you been clubbing long?"

She paused in the act of tugging her dress a few inches closer to her knees to consider his question. Frankly, she didn't know what he was talking about.

She'd felt that way all night, wondering what all of those young, brightly dressed people found so entertaining about the music blaring at them. Or the heat and crush of so many bodies pressed into such a small space.

But as soon as the girls at the beauty salon, who had cut, colored, blow-dried and spritzed her hair, found out her birthday plan to be wild and uninhibited for once in her sad, lonely life, they'd insisted she go to the most popular nightclub in town and pick up a hot guy. She suspected they would enjoy her predicament a little more than she was, but had to admit she wouldn't have gotten half as far without them.

They'd also done her nails and makeup, then directed her to a boutique down the street where a tall, black woman with fuchsia highlights in her hair had put her in this strapless black dress and four-inch stiletto heels.

"I can tell by your lack of response that you haven't been on the scene all that long," he said wryly, opening the door of the bright-yellow taxi that pulled up, then handing her inside.

Watching him slide into the backseat beside her, Gwen frowned. So much for being wild. She couldn't even keep up with today's vocabulary.

That realization and the knowledge that this handsome, sophisticated man had found her out made tears well in her eyes.

"Hey, take it easy."

He reached over and brushed the moisture from beneath her eye with his thumb. His blue sports jacket opened with the movement, giving her a better view of his chest, broad and well defined beneath a tight black T-shirt. The sight, and his nearness, made her mouth go dry.

"I could tell you weren't a regular the minute I saw you," he continued. "But that doesn't mean you aren't welcome at The Hot Spot. I'm glad you came in to check the place out."

He followed that statement with a comforting, lopsided smile, and Gwen felt some of the tension ease from her limbs. He was being so nice to her. And if he'd told the truth about being the club's owner, he probably had better things to do than watch out for one lone, out-of-her-element patron. Even so, she was beginning to think she'd been lucky to be rescued by Ethan before she'd actually gone off with that other man in the terrible polyester suit.

What had she been thinking? she wondered

now. She wasn't *that* desperate to lose her virginity, was she?

"So where do you live, Gwen?" He tipped his head toward the driver. "I'll have him take you home."

The address was on the tip of her tongue, ready to spill out. But if she gave it to him, the taxi would go there, drop her off, and take Ethan back to the club. Her night would be over without a single act of recklessness. All of her efforts to find a new hairstyle, new clothes and supposedly new attitude would be for naught, and she would still be a thirty-one-year-old virgin.

The alcohol she'd consumed earlier threatened to revolt as panic seized her. "No!"

Ethan looked equal parts confused and amused by her outburst. "No?"

Meeting his gaze in the dim backseat of the cab, she shook her head. "I don't want to go home. I just got here, and it's my birthday, and I'm not going home until…"

"Until?"

Until I've done something wild, she thought. But what she said was, "Until I'm ready."

"Does that mean you want to go back inside?" he asked. "Because I don't think that's such a good idea. You've already had, what, two or three apple martinis? No offense, but it doesn't look like you could handle much more to drink. And the guy who tried to pick you up is still in there, so he'll probably just hit on you again. Do you really want to deal with that?"

No, she really didn't. But if she went home now, she would only curl up under the covers and cry herself to sleep. Then she would be so disappointed in herself, she might never get out of bed again.

Taking a deep breath and lifting her chin, she said, "I don't care. I'm not going home yet."

"If you don't want to go home, and you don't want to go back inside, where do you want to go?"

The idea popped into her head like magic and sent a shock of naughtiness skating down her spine. "To your place."

She watched his brows shoot up in surprise and thought she might just have a few bad-girl genes swimming around in her DNA, after all.

"My place," he repeated. "Are you sure about that?"

Gwen swallowed, holding his gaze. Her fingers tightened on the beaded clutch in her lap as she concentrated on her breathing to keep from hyperventilating. And then she nodded.

Ethan studied her for a long minute, inhaling the spicy scent of her perfume that wrapped itself around him and sent tendrils of longing straight to his groin.

It wouldn't be the first time he'd taken a woman home with him from the club, but he didn't usually set his sights on petite brunettes who got tipsy after only a couple of drinks. The women he hooked up with knew exactly what they were getting into and most times hung out at the club for just that purpose.

Still, there was something oddly intriguing about Gwen. About her walk, like a newborn giraffe, telling him she didn't wear heels that high very often. About the way she kept tugging at her short, black dress, as though she wasn't used to sexy clothes that showed off her nicely shaped derriere.

For whatever reason, he wasn't ready to be free of her company just yet.

Turning to the driver, who was sitting patiently in the front seat with the meter running, he said, "You heard her. We're going to my place." He gave the man his address and hoped he wasn't making a horrible mistake.

He let her into his apartment, then tossed the keys onto a nearby credenza, watching as she sashayed across the white shag carpet to the wide window overlooking the city. Lights sparkled and flashed on the black canvas like stars in a midnight sky.

"Can I get you a drink? Something nonalcoholic?" he asked.

She glanced over her shoulder and he was struck once again by how innocent she seemed. Even balancing on those stilts she called shoes, in her little dress, with her hair sprayed perfectly about her face…. She looked like any other club hopper who waltzed into the bar, but there was an air about her that said she wasn't nearly as experienced as she'd like people to think.

But then, the customers at The Hot Spot hung out there for any number of reasons. Some of them hoping to get lucky, some of them wanting to dance or drink, some just wanting to be part of a crowd so they wouldn't feel so alone. Why should Gwen be any different?

Why did he care?

He'd been asking himself that since they met, but still didn't have a decent answer.

"Yes, nothing alcoholic," she agreed softly, a small grin gracing her red-glossed lips. "Please."

"How about a soda?"

She inclined her head before turning back to the window.

After pouring them each a cola over ice, he moved behind her, handing her a glass over her shoulder. She took it and sipped.

"Happy birthday, by the way. Isn't that why you said you were at the club?"

Twisting to face him, she nodded. "I wanted to do something fun for a change."

"And did you? Have fun, I mean?"

She cocked her head and her brown eyes deepened by three shades, reminding him of rich, French-roast coffee or a bottle of dark, aged rum.

After several seconds her voice lowered to a whisper. "I don't know yet."

Lust tore through him at her words. White-hot and throbbing, it raised the temperature in the room and brought him to full, almost painful arousal.

Until now, he hadn't been thinking of her in those terms…or at least he'd been trying not to. But her meaning was unmistakable, and all his good intentions about being a nice guy, entertaining her for a while and then seeing her safely home flew out the window.

He swallowed hard, his fingers tightening around the cut glass tumbler. She was innocent. More innocent than most of the women he brought home from the club, at any rate. He needed to remember that and not take advantage of the situation.

Instead of scooping her up and carrying her to his bedroom the way he wanted, he took a long swallow of his drink, letting the carbonated soda tickle its way down his throat before gesturing to the couch.

"Would you like to sit down?"

For a moment he thought he saw disappointment flash across her delicate features before she moved past him toward the sofa. Ethan trailed behind, taking a seat beside her—close, but not too close—on the tan, overstuffed cushions.

"I like your apartment," she told him. Perched on the edge of the couch, she scanned the modern decor while worrying the cool glass of soda between her two small hands.

"Thank you."

The interior had a definite bachelor feel to it. But then, that was what he was, and what he'd asked for when he'd hired the decorator. White shag carpeting and a lot of black and chrome furniture filled the space. No homey, family-friendly furnishings for him. He'd gone that route once and gotten kicked in the teeth for his trouble.

"You're welcome to stay the night," he found himself saying, though he honestly couldn't figure out why. "I have a small guest room you can use. That is, if you still don't feel like going home tonight."

Her lashes fluttered as she raised her gaze to his. "I've already inconvenienced you enough for one night. I don't want to be a bother."

A stab of something close to regret hit him low in the gut. A minute ago it had sounded as if she was offering herself to him, but, like an idiot, he'd taken the high road and pretended to misunderstand her meaning. Now she was getting ready to leave and he suddenly didn't want her to go.

He opened his mouth to tell her so, but she beat him to the punch.

"There is one favor I'd like to ask of you," she said softly. So softly, he had to strain to hear. "If you wouldn't think I was being too forward."

He shook his head, eager to do anything that would keep her with him just a little longer. "What is it?"

Averting her eyes, she drew a deep breath. The tip of her tongue darted out to caress her full red lips, causing blood to rush to his already half-aroused manhood.

"Would you please kiss me?"

Two

Heat suffused Gwen's cheeks at her own audacity. Had she really just asked a virtual stranger to kiss her?

She'd meant to do something uninhibited for her birthday. But the way Ethan was looking at her, she had a feeling he thought her the biggest fool in Georgetown.

She lowered her head and started to set her glass on the low coffee table in front of the sofa, wanting nothing more than to escape from this man's apartment as fast as she could.

"I'm sorry," she said, unable to meet his gaze. "I shouldn't have asked that."

His hand darted out to grab her wrist as she began to rise.

"Wait. Don't go. And don't apologize," he said, urging her back down to the sofa. "You just caught me off guard there for a minute. I've been sitting here telling myself not to stare at your mouth or wonder what you look like naked. I was determined to be a gentleman and offer you a place to stay for the night—a place other than my bed, mind you," he added with a wry grin. "So the last thing I expected was for you to come right out and ask me to kiss you."

Gwen shook her head. "I'm sorry, I shouldn't have—"

"Hey." He took her chin between a thumb and forefinger, turning her to face him. "I told you, no apologizing. Kissing a beautiful woman isn't exactly a hardship, you know."

His words slid like drawn butter through her veins. No one had ever called her beautiful before, and whether she believed him or not, he'd made her *feel* beautiful.

After taking a deep breath, she licked her lips and stared into his green-flecked eyes. "So are you going to? Kiss me, I mean?"

His lips quirked up in amusement. "Yeah, I'm going to kiss you. Just…give me a minute, okay?"

Her stomach flipped over in anticipation, her lungs struggling for air as she watched him watching her.

Why wouldn't he kiss her? What was he waiting for? Was she doing something wrong?

Maybe he didn't like to kiss women who had their eyes open. She'd sort of wanted to see what was happening. He was so handsome, and this meant so much to her. But if closing her eyes would get him to put his lips on hers that much sooner, then she would do it.

Letting her lashes drift closed, she shimmied closer to him on the overstuffed sofa cushions and tipped her head back, mouth pursed in preparation. She felt his breath on her face and shivered.

"Gwen."

His voice, at such close proximity, vibrated across her skin.

"Open your eyes."

She followed his direction without conscious thought, eyes popping open to find him *right there,* his mouth hovering centimeters above her own. And then, before her brain could process anything more, he was kissing her.

His lips were like velvet, pressing and caressing while his tongue traced the line of her mouth before plunging inside.

Gwen had been kissed before; she'd even insti-gated kissing a time or two. But never in her life had she been kissed like this. Never before had the mere meeting of lips stopped her heart or sent heat pool-ing between her legs.

As gentle as Ethan was, he still devoured her, turning her inside out with the stroke of his tongue, the mastery of his lips.

When he finally released her, she slumped back against the arm of the sofa, breathing hard.

Wow. She'd heard the old adage "Be careful what you wish for, you just might get it" but never realized it could be applied to the good as well as the bad.

Who was she kidding? That kiss hadn't been just good, it had been phenomenal. Her insides were still quivering and her lips were actually numb, at least around the edges.

One glance at Ethan and she knew he wasn't entirely unaffected, either. His chest rose and fell in quick bursts beneath the electric-blue silk of his jacket, and his unblinking eyes seemed riveted on her mouth.

She swallowed convulsively, letting her tongue dart out to lick the taste of him from her lips. If possible, his gaze turned even darker and hotter, threatening to singe her sensitive flesh.

"Would you think I was a terrible person if I said I'd like to do that again?" she asked, surprised she could find the courage to voice such a question.

"No," he answered without hesitation, "but you might be a mind reader."

He moved his hand up to brush the side of her face, and she tilted her head, leaning into the gentleness of his touch.

She'd never felt this sense of longing before, of

wanting to wrap herself around another human being and never let go. Of having that man wrap himself around her.

And suddenly she knew if she left this apartment without making love to Ethan Banks…without letting him make love to her…she would never forgive herself.

"After you kiss me again," she said slowly, lifting her hand to cover his where it still rested against her cheek, "do you think you might be willing to make love to me, too?"

Desire hit Ethan in the solar plexus hard enough to drive the oxygen from his lungs. He must have died and gone to heaven. Or he was sleeping and having one of the best fantasies he'd ever imagined.

She was offering herself to him, and he wanted nothing more than to accept. He couldn't remember a time when he'd been this turned on.

But even so, he felt an insane need to protect Gwen …or at least give her a chance to change her mind before he dragged her down to the floor and buried himself in her warm, welcoming sweetness.

"Gwen." He let his fingers slide over her soft skin, down the column of her throat, to the small jut of her delicate collarbone. "You're a beautiful woman, but—"

Her hand shot out to cover his mouth, stopping him in mid-sentence.

"Please," she whispered, glossy brown eyes meeting his. "Don't say no. Unless you're not attracted to me. I'll understand if you aren't."

The last was said on a rush, her gaze sliding away in embarrassment.

"It's not that," he was quick to correct her. *"Believe me,* it's not that."

"Then…maybe you could consider it a birthday present and just try. For me."

A dry laugh gurgled its way up his throat, getting stuck midway and nearly choking him.

Try? Consider it a birthday present?

Did she have any idea how hard he was trying right now to be noble? Or how difficult she was making it for him?

Would he make love to her?

Hell, yes.

Would he—or, worse, she—regret it in the morning?

Maybe.

At the moment, though, he honestly didn't care. Whatever the repercussions, he'd deal with them. Later.

He slid closer to her on the sofa, until his knees bracketed one of her black silk-clad legs. Running his fingers through her hair, he tucked a strand behind her ear and gave her what he hoped was a benign smile.

"I want you to be sure about this, Gwen. I want it to be you talking and not the two or three appletinis you drank at the club."

"It was only two," she answered, her eyes very clear and alert as she stared back at him. "And I'm very, very sure."

Thank God, he thought, swallowing a lump of anticipation he hadn't realized was lodged in his throat.

With a nod, he rose to his feet and pulled her up after him.

He'd thought about taking her right there on the sofa, or maybe on the carpet in front of the sofa. But it was Gwen's birthday, and as much as he wanted her, he thought a little finesse might be called for rather than desperate groping in the middle of the living room.

"Come on," he said, leading her through the rest of the apartment to his bedroom.

He expected her to look around, take in the rest of the decor. Instead, her gaze remained on his as he walked backward toward their final destination. He kept their fingers linked, rubbing his thumbs over the soft skin of her knuckles.

It was an odd intimacy for him. Usually, he and the women he brought home from the club simply got down to business.

For some reason, though, he wanted to take things more slowly tonight. He wanted to pull back the covers and invite Gwen into his bed, then watch her undress. Or maybe undress her himself.

When they reached his bedroom, he waited for her

vision to adjust to the darker surroundings. When it did, her gaze raked over his king-size bed with navy-blue satin coverlet to match the padded headboard.

"I've never seen such a big bed before."

One side of his mouth lifted. "You'll like it," he told her. He'd make sure of it.

She stood perfectly still in the center of the room, staring at the bed as though it had teeth and was about to bite her.

"Don't be nervous, Gwen. We'll go as slow as you want."

She blinked, once, then turned to look at him. "I'm not nervous. I just…don't know where to start."

Stepping in front of her, his back to the bed, he put his hands on her shoulders and gently stroked her bare skin. "Why don't we start with another kiss? The first one turned out pretty well, don't you think?"

He gave her a wry grin and was rewarded with a slight tilt of her lips in return.

Lowering his head, he brushed her mouth lightly with his lips, then let his tongue trail almost imperceptibly along the seam. He felt the tension flee her body in one great sigh as she leaned against him, her nails clutching his upper arms.

Her lips parted and she threw herself wholly into the kiss, biting, sucking, exploring. Drawing him deeper and deeper until a groan rolled its way up from low in his belly.

If there had been any doubts in his mind before about making love to Gwen, he certainly didn't harbor them now. She was pressed too close, kissing him too passionately not to be a willing participant.

Continuing their kiss, he shifted his footing until he'd turned her back to the big bed frame. Her knees buckled when they bumped the edge of the mattress, and he caught her, slowly lowering her to a sitting position on the silky coverlet.

The move broke their heavy lip-lock and they both sat back, breathing hard. Gwen stared at him with dark, glazed-over eyes, and Ethan suspected his would look much the same if he took the time to glance in the mirror.

This woman did things to him. Made his heart beat faster. Made the blood thicken in his veins. Brought him to a state of almost painful arousal.

He could only hope he had a similar effect on her. From the expression on her face, he would say he did, but the blasted black dress she was wearing made it hard to discern any other physical reactions.

Sinking to one knee on the carpeted floor, he held her gaze while his hands circled her slim ankles. The padded tips of his fingers rubbed sensually over the silk of her stockings, moving slowly upward.

Her chest hitched as she breathed, filling the modest cups of her strapless dress even fuller. How he wanted to taste her there. Kiss her skin, watch her nipples bud with desire. Would they be large and dark like raspberries or small and pink like cherry blossom buds?

He slid his palms behind her shins to gently caress her calves, then back over to her knees, across her thighs, with his thumbs riding just inside, closer and closer to her feminine center. Beneath the high hem of her short black dress, his fingers encountered the smooth warmth of bare flesh.

A shudder tore through him. She was wearing actual stockings rather than panty hose, complete with little snaps that, he hoped, attached to an equally minuscule garter belt. Something lacy and racy and black. Or maybe red…a seductive contrast to the solid black of her outfit.

Suddenly he wanted to see her in her undergarments. He'd intended to peel her out of her shoes and hose, working his way up to the zipper of her dress. But now he decided to change tactics.

Climbing to his feet, he pulled her up in front of him and offered a reassuring smile. "Let's go at this a little differently, shall we?"

She looked timid and a little nervous, but after a second she nodded.

To put her more at ease, Ethan shrugged out of his jacket, tossing it aside in the direction of a big, overstuffed armchair tucked in the corner of the room. Next, he kicked off his shoes and unbuckled his belt, pulling the polished leather slowly through the loops at his waist.

He stopped there, not wanting to intimidate her by stripping down completely while she was still fully dressed. Instead he reached out to finger the zipper at the side of her dress.

"Do you mind?" he asked.

She glanced down, watching his dark fingers toy with the cool metal. Then she lifted her head and once again met his gaze, tipping her head in the affirmative.

That was all it took for him to release the eye hook. Inch by inch, he unzipped the tight dress, coming closer and closer to exposing the soft swell of her delicate bosom.

The dress finally fell free, revealing smooth, porcelain flesh and the cups of a feminine, lace-covered strapless demibra.

He took a deep breath to steady his quickly evaporating control and stepped back. "My turn."

Crossing his arms over his chest and abdomen, he grabbed the bottom of his cotton T-shirt and pulled it up and over his head. Then he slipped the button at the top of his pants through its hole and slowly lowered the zipper over his straining manhood.

He didn't want to frighten Gwen, but he planned to get her naked in short order and thought it might be prudent to be a little ahead of the game before they reached that point.

After removing his tailored slacks, he stood before her in nothing more than a pair of black briefs, made all the tighter by his aroused condition.

The minute Ethan had shrugged out of his fitted cotton shirt, Gwen's mouth went sandpaper dry. And now that he was all but nude, save his underwear, she was having trouble drawing air into her petrified lungs. Lack of oxygen and the fine male specimen standing before her were making her feel light-headed.

She'd never seen anyone as handsome as Ethan Banks, not even in the movies. His chest was a study of lightly bronzed lines and planes, with only a slight dusting of hair covering his otherwise smooth pectorals.

He must work out, she thought, given the bulging muscles of his upper arms and the firm definition of his abdomen. His hips were narrow, his thighs wide and strong, but what drew her eye like an electrical current was the large bulge straining against the front of his briefs.

It awed her to know she'd caused such a reaction. That he was turned on and unashamed to let her see just how much.

Curiosity ate at her. She wanted to reach out and touch him, run her hands over all that warm, sun-kissed skin and feel the throbbing pressure of his erection.

Would he mind? Was she allowed to touch him the

way he'd touched her when he'd run his hands up her legs and nearly turned them to jelly?

She was about to ask, or at least step closer, when he beat her to the punch and moved closer to slide his fingers under the waist of her dress.

"Unfair advantage," he murmured. "If I'm going to be half-naked, I want you half-naked, too."

Holding her gaze, he slid the stretchy material over her hips and let the dress fall in a pool at her feet. Then he lowered his gaze to the garter belt and minuscule wisp of silk the woman at the boutique insisted were panties.

She had never worn anything so tiny or transparent in her life, but the saleslady had insisted the panties went with the bra and garter belt. And since she was being beyond daring with the strapless black dress, Gwen had decided to go all the way.

Now she was glad she had. Her skin flushed hot at the knowledge that her underthings didn't so much cover her private areas as provide a thin veil through which they could be viewed. But the look on Ethan's face when he stared at her barely covered body made even that small amount of embarrassment worth it.

He licked his lips once and then dragged his gaze back up to hers. "Remind me to send a note to Victoria in the morning thanking her for sharing her secrets with the rest of the world."

Her lips tipped up at his obvious pleasure in her undergarments. "That's not where I got them, but I'm sure the woman who owns the shop would be happy to hear you like them."

"*Like* is a vast understatement. Before the night is through, I intend to give them my five-star stamp of approval. Of course, at least two of those stars depend on just how easy they are to remove."

He licked his lips again, and a shaft of desire strong enough to bring her to her knees shot through her.

"Care to find out?"

She nodded weakly, her breath coming in shallow pants because her muscles were bunched too tight to allow her lungs proper expansion.

Ethan lowered himself to one knee in front of her, taking his time, letting his fingers graze the lace tops of her stockings before giving a little flick and setting the front two snaps free. She gasped as the elastic bands holding her stockings in place snapped upward and stung her.

"Sorry," he offered, but the wicked glint in his eyes and small lift at the corner of his mouth told her he wasn't really sorry at all.

Flattening his palms on her upper thighs, he ran them slowly around to her backside, giving the plump flesh a squeeze as he released the second set of fasteners. He didn't even try to keep the bands from snapping up and stinging her on the behind, grinning when she yelped and her body jerked with surprise.

"That wasn't very nice," she chastised breathlessly.

"No," he said, still smiling, "but this will be."

And with that he reached out to lick a trail from the top of her right stocking to the thin string holding her panties in place. Fire leaped beneath her skin, all but raising steam where his tongue had touched her.

"Oh, my," she sighed, her knees shaking as she fought to remain standing.

She was definitely in over her head.

Three

Gwen had never gone to bed with a man before, and now, when she finally decided to change that sorry state of affairs, she'd picked a man who could nearly bring her to orgasm with one look, one touch, one slip of his tongue over her naked flesh. Her belly quivered in anticipation of what he might do next—if she remained conscious long enough to find out.

His breath brought goose bumps to the surface of her skin as he took the delicate silk of the hose between his teeth and dragged it down, down, down.

Her diaphragm hitched. Her throat closed. Sensations she'd never even dreamed possible swirled behind her eyes in a kaleidoscope of colors.

She clutched at his shoulders, afraid of losing her balance or passing out from sheer delight while he peeled the stocking down her leg and over her heel, then shifted to repeat the excruciating process on her other leg.

When he finished, he lifted his head and tucked his thumbs under the waist of the now-useless garter belt.

"I hope you enjoyed that as much as I did," he told her, his voice low and gravelly with pent-up passion.

Gwen swallowed hard and inclined her head, relieved that he seemed just as affected by his ministrations as she was.

Her nails still dug into his arms like talons, when, in one fluid movement, he pushed the belt and panties down to her ankles. She'd expected to feel nervous or even frightened when the time came to finally stand naked in front of this man, but instead she felt oddly calm. The black strapless bra was still firmly in place, but he'd already bared the most intimate part of her body.

Lifting her leg, she stepped back and used her other foot to kick the panties out of the way. Then, reaching behind her, she unhooked the bra and let it fall from her fingertips to the floor.

She heard him suck a breath through his teeth and almost mimicked the action when he put his hands on her waist and pushed to his feet. His chest rubbed the pointed tips of her breasts, his lower extremities bumping suggestively against her own—deliberately, she was sure.

"Keep doing things like that, sweetheart, and I won't last very long."

Since she'd never done this before, she didn't really have any sort of timetable to go by. But considering how her skin tingled and her insides turned to molten lava whenever he touched her, she suspected she might not be far behind.

With little effort, he lifted her off her feet and deposited her in the middle of the wide bed. After skimming his underwear down over his hips, he took two long strides to the black lacquer nightstand and opened a drawer.

Thank goodness he had protection, Gwen thought when she saw the foil packet, along with the forethought to get it out at the right moment. For someone who'd gone out this evening with the sole hope of finding a man to relieve her of her virginity, she certainly hadn't done a very good job of planning ahead.

Which was one more reason to be grateful she'd left with Ethan instead of that other fellow who'd tried to pick her up.

She also didn't think the man in the leisure suit would have looked half this good naked. Having never seen a man without his clothes on before,

Gwen ignored her natural inclination toward modesty and looked her fill.

His broad chest tapered to narrow hips with an arrow of dark hair leading the eye directly to the root of his manhood. He was fully aroused.

The mattress sank with his weight as he crawled toward her, then straightened to tear open the small foil square with his teeth before rolling the condom down his turgid length. Her fingers curled into the coverlet at her back as wonder and anticipation coursed through her veins. He lowered himself over her, pressing against her from chest to ankle, and every thought in her head vanished like smoke from an extinguished candlewick.

Ethan ran his fingers through the hair at her temple. "Are you okay?"

She nodded, even though it was far from the truth. She was hot and achy, curious and eager, a little nervous. Anything but merely *okay*.

He smiled before leaning in to take her mouth. Her lips parted, inviting him to deepen the kiss, take her tongue, nip and suck and bite.

Her arms roped around his neck, holding him close, while his hands snaked down then up her body. He stopped to cup his palms around her breasts, teasing the pebbled peaks with his thumbs.

Letting his lips leave hers, he trailed a row of kisses along her chin, the column of her neck and the gentle slope of her chest. With his tongue, he teased first one nipple and then the other, the cool air raising goose bumps on her dampened skin.

She arched her back in pleasure, offering up her breasts for his sinful ministrations. Emboldened, he licked a circle around the distended area of her areola and then sucked the nipple into his mouth.

Sensations overwhelmed her, the nerve endings behind her breast sending signals of delight coursing through her body. Her fingers curled into fists at her sides, bunching the satiny bedclothes.

He repeated the wicked onslaught on her other breast until she thought she'd go mad. Then his mouth whispered away from her chest, moving lower to her ribs and belly.

His tongue did laps around her navel, swirling, licking, rasping like a kitten's on her overly sensitive skin. And then it dipped inside for just a second before moving even lower.

Embarrassment swamped her as his warm breath blew over the curls between her legs, which she tried almost desperately to clamp together. He ignored her feeble protest, pushing her thighs apart again so that he could explore her feminine secrets with his mouth and hands.

His fingertips ran along both sides of the slick flesh before holding her open and taking one long swipe with his tongue.

It was like being touched with a live electrical wire in a very private place. She gave a small mewl of surprise and her hips came up off the bed.

While his mouth and tongue worshipped her, Ethan slipped one long, broad finger into her narrow passage. Gwen gasped and felt herself tighten around him without conscious thought.

She bore down on her heels, lifting her pelvis closer to the pleasure she sensed only he could give her. Sliding a second finger into her, he started to thrust, his tongue zeroing in on the swollen bud where every cell in her body that carried sensations back to her brain seemed to be located.

Without warning, she flew apart. Crying out, she clutched at his hair. And like a plane flying too close to the sun, she burst into flames, returning to earth in charred little pieces.

Her chest heaved as he levered himself back up and over her. He stared down into her face for a moment, and then smiled.

"I hope you enjoyed that."

She parted her lips to reply, but no words came out. Her mouth had gone completely dry, and she still felt as if she was floating somewhere outside the planet's atmosphere.

"Good," he murmured in a low, seductive voice. "Now I have an even better idea."

Catching her behind the knees, he lifted her legs

to wrap behind his waist. She felt the firm, persistent prodding of his erection at the opening of her womanhood, and for a moment it struck her that she should be afraid. After all, they hadn't actually done *the* deed yet, despite the liberties he'd just taken with her body.

But she wanted this. She wanted him. And everything he did to her only made her want him more.

If there was pain or discomfort from the actual act, she would deal with it. It couldn't last that long, anyway.

And then he was inside her, nudging forward, the wide, hot pressure of him stretching her sensitive inner passageway. He moved slowly, but she still caught her breath, her body arching and then remaining rigid until he was lodged fully between her thighs.

"Relax, Gwen," Ethan whispered softly.

He pushed the hair back from her damp brow and she opened her eyes, not even realizing she'd had them clamped tightly closed.

It didn't hurt. She wasn't sure why she'd been expecting it to…unless it was all the stories she'd heard about women losing their virginity. Stories involving tears and blood.

But she wasn't crying. She didn't think she was bleeding, either. And she wasn't in pain, she only felt…full. Filled, for the very first time in her life, with an intimate part of Ethan.

"Better now?" he asked, watching her intently.

"Yes." How could she not be when he was being so gentle and accommodating? She'd heard stories, about men who rushed and groped and fumbled, and didn't much care whether their partners were enjoying themselves or not.

Luckily, Ethan wasn't at all like that. He was slow and patient and attentive, always concerned about her pleasure and comfort. Yes, she could have done much, much worse.

Suddenly, keeping still beneath him seemed almost unbearable. She needed to move, needed him to move inside her and ease the terrible ache that was throbbing low in her belly.

Raking her nails down the slick slope of his back, she hiked her knees even higher on his hips and crossed her ankles, locking him in place against the cradle of her pelvis.

With a groan, he raised up on his forearms and began to stroke. Forward, then back. Up a little, then down, causing a delicious friction between their bodies.

Heat and moisture built as he increased his rhythm, and Gwen found herself rocking her hips, lifting to meet each powerful thrust. Her head dug into the mattress as Ethan kissed her ear, the pulse in her neck, the crest of her breast. Her breathing came in tandem with the beating of her heart and she heard the mewling sounds she was making at the back of her throat.

With one hand, he toyed with the nipple he'd already brought to sharp arousal. But when his other hand slipped into the wet heat of her feminine folds to tease the tiny bud of her desire, skyrockets went off in her bloodstream, and her mouth opened to scream his name.

Ethan continued to thrust, drawing her hips up to meet each pounding of pleasure until he, too, stiffened above her and came on a loud groan.

Little by little, her heartbeat slowed and returned to normal. Ethan's heavy, prone body rested atop her, pressing her into the mattress, but she liked it. She liked the feel of his arms and legs tangled with her own, his chest rising and falling against her as he dragged air into his deprived lungs, his slightly stubbled jaw rubbing the side of her face as he turned his head to look at her.

"That was amazing," he said, still somewhat breathless. "We'll definitely be doing that again— just as soon as I recover."

A wide grin split her face. She couldn't wait to make love with him again, but even more, it delighted her to know he'd enjoyed their encounter as much as she had. And he must have, if he was already anticipating a repeat performance.

Before she lost her nerve, she grabbed him by the ears, lifted her head and kissed him smack on the lips.

"Thank you," she said. For taking my virginity…for being my first…for making me feel so wonderful, like a mature, sensual woman.

He stared at her for a long, silent moment, and then his lips quirked in an answering smile. "It was my pleasure, believe me."

Rotating his hips, he groaned as she bit her lip and tipped her own pelvis to meet him.

"And in a minute, it will be my pleasure again."

Oh, she didn't doubt it for a minute. Already he began to swell within her.

How did he do it? How did he turn her from a timid introvert to a wanton extrovert? The transformation might not last once she left his bed, but for now she was the wild, uninhibited soul she'd always dreamed of being.

The next time Gwen opened her eyes, early-morning sunlight streamed across the room. At first, she suffered a sense of panicked confusion at the strangeness of her surroundings and the weight of another body pressing against her side.

And then it all came rushing back. Her birthday, the makeover, the club…Ethan.

A flush of heat stained her cheeks at the memory of what they'd done together. Even so, her heart thrilled at the knowledge that she could finally shed the moniker of boring, mousy, *virgin* librarian.

Two of those adjectives might still be true, but the third definitely was not. Not after last night.

Slipping out from under the warm sheet and even warmer arm Ethan had draped across her stomach, she shimmied from the bed and began a silent but frantic search for her clothes. She stepped into her panties and zipped up her dress, but stuffed as much of the bra and stockings into her beaded clutch as would fit rather than take the time to get completely redressed.

Ethan was still sound asleep, and for a moment Gwen considered climbing back into bed so she could be there when he woke up.

But then what? They might make love again—the thought caused her knees to weaken—but eventually he would want to get up and have breakfast and probably…talk.

She'd achieved her goal last night with a couple of drinks in her system and not much conversation. She was very much afraid she'd reverted to her frumpy, unexciting self sometime before morning, like Cinderella at the stroke of midnight.

Trying to pretend she was experienced in the bright light of day was too much for her and she worried Ethan would immediately see through her facade. And if he found out who she really was, then the fantasy she'd been allowed to live for a few short hours would disappear, replaced with the look of shock and disappointment that was sure to fill his face.

No, better for her to leave now, before he awoke and she turned back into a frog—in his eyes, at least.

Stiletto heels dangling from her fingertips, she tiptoed down the hall, her movements silenced by the deep pile carpeting. When she spotted a small notepad next to the phone on the kitchen counter, she hesitated and then decided to scrawl a short note for Ethan to find when he woke up.

Leaving the slip of paper where he'd be most likely to see it, she quietly snicked open both the chain and dead bolt on the front door, and sneaked away.

With a wide yawn, Ethan stretched and came slowly awake.

God, he felt good. It had been a long time since he'd woken up feeling so refreshed.

Probably had something to do with Gwen wearing him out.

The corners of his mouth curved upward as he remembered the warm flush of her petal-soft skin, the awe in her eyes, and all the things they'd done throughout the night.

As a rule, he didn't let women sleep in his bed. He'd bring them home with him, but as soon as they were finished, he would see them home or see them back to the club.

But last night, with Gwen… The thought of asking her to leave had never entered his mind. If anything, he'd been ready to invent reasons for her to stay if she even tried to run off. And after their second or third bout of mind-blowing ecstasy, he'd been more than content to drift off with her tucked securely in his arms.

Maybe he'd be lucky enough to interest her in another round this morning.

He ran his palm across the mattress, letting his eyes drift open as he waited for his fingers to tangle through her soft auburn hair or brush against the swell of one of her small, pert breasts. But she wasn't there.

He blinked to clear his vision and searched the bed, only to realize she was no longer beside him. Sitting up, he saw the clothes he'd discarded last night lying haphazardly on the floor and tossed over the arm of a chair, but Gwen's garments were missing.

He smiled. Obviously she'd woken up before he had and gone into the kitchen in search of breakfast. His own stomach was rumbling, telling him that wasn't such a bad idea.

Rolling to his feet, he walked naked to the glossy black bureau, removed a pair of paisley satin pajama bottoms, and stepped into them. The elastic waistband snapped into place low on his hips as he padded barefoot out of the bedroom toward the living and kitchen areas.

He paused at the end of the short hallway, listening for signs of Gwen's presence. The opening and closing of a cupboard door, the scrape of utensils on china, the pop of the toaster. But he was met with an almost eerie silence. If she was here, she was being as quiet as a ghost.

But she was gone.

After his search of the apartment, he returned to the kitchen to brew a pot of coffee.

It was a shame Gwen hadn't stuck around; they might have had some fun this morning. He could have taken her out for breakfast or regaled her with his cooking skills by whipping up one of his famous western omelets. Not to mention luring her back to the bedroom.

When he noticed the sheet of paper lying on the countertop, a stab of regret went through him, followed swiftly by annoyance.

Thanks for making my birthday special.

She hadn't even signed the note.

Ethan cursed as he crumpled the paper in his fist and threw it in the general direction of the trash can. It bounced off the wall and rolled under the cabinet.

Why was this bothering him so much? Normally he was glad to wake up to an empty apartment, relieved not to have to muddle through awkward niceties.

But she could have said good-bye in person. At the very least she could have given him her phone number or told him where she lived. How was he supposed to find her again without anything more personal to go by than her name?

Whoa.

Find her again? Did he even intend to look? He never had before, had never felt the need to see a woman other than his ex-wife more than once. But there was something about Gwen that got under his skin, made him want to know more.

It didn't help, either, that she'd been a virgin. She might not think he'd noticed, but he had. She'd been tight, and when he'd slid into her all the way, he'd felt her stiffen and watched her bite down gently on her bottom lip to keep from crying out.

He wondered why she hadn't told him before things had gone too far. He hadn't been rough with her by any means, but he might have been a little more gentle if he'd known. Taken things a little more slowly.

And then he wondered if that hadn't been the point all along. Was that what she'd meant by thanking him for making her birthday special?

She'd almost left The Hot Spot with that polyester lizard, and then seemed more than happy to let Ethan rescue her and take her home. Had that been her plan from the start? To hook up with some stranger who would be more than happy to relieve her of her virginity?

He wasn't certain of her age, but she looked too old never to have been with a man before. Especially with that body, that hair, that taste in watch-me-want-me-take-me fashion.

But if his suspicions were correct...

He felt used.

Funny, for a man who'd had his share of one-night stands. He couldn't say he liked the feeling one damn bit.

Digging Gwen's balled-up note out from under the row of cabinets, he peeled it open and ran the heel of his hand over the thin, white square to smooth the wrinkles.

So maybe he would look for her. There were some choice questions he'd like to ask the next time he ran into her, and she was bound to return to the club eventually. He'd simply put his staff on the lookout for a petite redhead with soft chocolate eyes and a laugh that could melt a man's bones.

With that thought in mind, he put the abandoned pot of coffee on to drip, then headed back to the bedroom to take a shower and dress. If he went into the club early today, he'd be able to get some paperwork done, as well as talk to each of his employees as they arrived for work about keeping an eye out for Gwen.

He'd find her, and then the two of them would have a little talk.

Four

Two weeks passed with no sign of Gwen at The Hot Spot, and Ethan became more surly by the day.

Just last night, before closing, he'd snapped at one of his waitresses simply because she brought him a Scotch on the rocks when he'd asked for it straight up…and because she had the audacity to wear her highlighted auburn hair in a style that reminded him of Gwen's.

This had to stop, he thought, pounding on the steering wheel in frustration. It was obvious she wasn't going to sashay into his bar anytime soon, considering she hadn't found it necessary to do so in the past thirteen days, four hours and twenty-seven minutes.

Which meant he either had to forget her or take other measures to track her down.

Well, if he were honest, he had tried to forget her.

He'd done some drinking—not all that much more than his usual social drinking, but enough that his staff had started to cast strange looks in his direction.

He'd gone to the gym with his best friend, Peter, and tried to work off his frustrations—first on the treadmill, then with free weights, and finally by knocking the stuffing out of a punching bag while Peter held the heavy piece of equipment and bit his tongue to keep from asking for the dozenth time what had crawled up Ethan's butt and died.

None of it helped.

And worst of all, he hadn't had sex, since Gwen effectively eliminated his desire for any other woman.

Oh, women at the club had flirted with him whenever he left his office long enough to be seen at the bar. He'd even flirted back a bit…until he realized it was more out of habit than from any real interest in taking the women home with him.

What he needed was to get laid. Tension and a low ebb of anger coursed through his body twenty-four/seven, and the only way he could think to rid himself of the jaw-clenching emotions was to achieve physical release.

Unfortunately, the only person he wanted to attain

that relief with was a certain petite redhead by the name of Gwen Thomas.

As though reflection alone caused her to materialize from thin air, he spotted her on the steps of the local library.

At least, he thought it was Gwen.

He stood on the brakes, belatedly realizing he was in the middle of the heavy midday traffic crawling through downtown Georgetown. Lifting his foot, he just managed to avoid being rear-ended by the car behind him.

He returned his gaze to the library.

Now where the hell was she? Had he lost her again already?

No, wait, there she was, walking down the street.

He craned his neck to keep her in sight until he was able to edge out of the lunch hour crush and into an available parking space.

Jumping out of his silver Lexus, he poured a handful of change into the meter and raced down the street, desperately trying to keep an eye trained on the woman he suspected was Gwen.

She looked different. Her hair was a deep brunette instead of the lighter auburn he remembered, falling to her shoulders in waves rather than being teased off her face.

Her clothes, too, were more reserved. Whereas the black dress she'd worn had wrapped around her like a second skin, showing off every dip and curve of her body to perfection, the dress she wore today was long and loose, with tiny flowers dancing across a vanilla background. It flowed about her calves in the slight breeze, drawing his attention to the pair of flat-soled, reddish-brown sandals on her feet.

She seemed…earthier, more simplistic this way. Surprisingly, Ethan didn't find the change any less attractive.

He had nearly caught up to her now, but kept his distance, wanting to be sure this was actually Gwen and not just someone who looked incredibly similar to her. He was also curious to know where she was going, and the only way he would find out was to follow her there.

Six or eight blocks later, she turned into the doorway of a large, brown brick building. Pausing in the spot she'd occupied just a moment ago, he glanced up and saw that it was an apartment complex, then darted inside before the plate glass security door could click shut.

After passing a bank of mailboxes on his right, he started up the mahogany stairwell, keeping his tread light as he listened for the soft squeak of Gwen's footsteps above him. He took his time, not wanting to catch up with her too soon.

At the third-floor landing he heard her pace change and he took the stairs two at a time so he could see which apartment she entered. In profile, as he watched her turn the key in the lock, she looked very much like the Gwen he knew, despite the changes in her appearance.

His blood thickened, pumping harder through his veins at the thought of being close to her again. He only hoped she'd be happy to see him…which was questionable, considering the way she'd left his apartment and never attempted to contact him again.

Which made him wonder—not for the first time— why he was so obsessed with tracking her down. He hoped it was merely a case of wounded pride, since she was the only woman he'd ever been with who hadn't tried to wiggle even more deeply into his life.

The minute she disappeared inside the apartment, he started forward and lifted a hand to rap on the door.

Gwen jumped in the process of making a sand-wich for her lunch, startled by the loud knock at her apartment door. She hardly ever got visitors, and couldn't imagine anyone she knew pounding with such authority.

Mr. Gonzalez, her landlord, was a big man, but she doubted he would be calling, since she hadn't reported any problems with her plumbing lately. And kindly Mrs. Snedden at the end of the hall tapped lightly when she came over, usually in the evenings when she had a casserole or fresh-baked pastry she wanted to share.

Wiping a smear of mayonnaise from her finger with a dishrag, she set her sandwich fixings aside and moved the short distance to look through the peephole. As soon as she saw who was standing on the other side of the door, her heart froze in her chest.

Oh, my God, it was he.

How had he found her?

What did he want?

She glanced down at herself and realized how dowdy she looked.

Nothing like the sex kitten Ethan had met that night at the club.

Although she'd loved the freedom and self-assurance her makeover had brought her, she quickly realized she couldn't continue to carry off such a look in her everyday life. Her colleagues at the library would fall over in a dead faint if she changed too much too fast, so she'd gone for subtle adjustments instead.

Her wardrobe was one of them. It was slightly updated now—she found herself enjoying the shopping experience more than she had before—and she took the time each morning to mix and match different pieces to create a new outfit.

Her hair was another. She'd had the girl at the salon change the red coloring back to brown, but a darker, lusher tone than her natural shade. And she thought the new cut framed her face well, even without all the teasing and hairspray the stylist had insisted on using for that first, monumental birthday makeover.

Still, she couldn't let Ethan see her like this. He would think he'd landed at the door of Gwen's geekier twin sister.

Sucking in a deep breath, she darted farther into the apartment and tried not to let her voice waver as she called out, "Who is it?"

A beat passed before his muffled response permeated the thick wooden panel. "Ethan. Ethan Banks. I'm looking for Gwen…um, Gwen Thomas."

The familiar deep timbre of his voice raised goose bumps along her flesh. As stunned as she was by his unexpected appearance at her door, a part of her was thrilled that he'd gone to the bother of tracking her down, and suddenly she was eager to talk with him again.

"Ethan! What a surprise," she returned, backing toward her bedroom. "Give me a minute, would you? I'll be right out."

She kicked out of her sandals and tore off her dress in record time, digging through her closet for something Ethan might think more appropriate for the woman he thought her to be.

She settled for a pair of tight white jeans and a pink, off-the-shoulder knit top with a big flower in the same material adorning one breast. These newest additions to her wardrobe proved she did actually possess a feminine form, even if it was a bit on the petite side.

Long silver teardrop earrings and a pair of pink pumps completed what she hoped was a decent outfit. Not quite as revealing as Ethan might be expecting, but a definite change from what she'd worn to work that morning.

Hurrying back through the kitchen, she paused a moment to get her skittering nerve endings under control and then opened the door just enough to peek out.

Lord, he was even more handsome than she remembered. His dark hair was carelessly disheveled, as though he'd run his fingers through it a few dozen times while waiting. His hazel eyes were narrowed and suspicious, but otherwise he looked completely relaxed. He was wearing hunter-green chinos with a matching jacket and a tan button-down shirt beneath.

Good enough to eat, as some of the teenage girls who were occasional patrons of the library might say.

"Ethan. Hi," she greeted him a bit breathlessly, careful to keep one foot propped on the other side of the door so he couldn't see too far into the apartment.

Her floral-print sofa, muted eggshell walls and collection of ceramic cat figurines didn't exactly scream "wild woman." And she was afraid that if he came inside, he would realize what a sham her whole personality was—at least the personality she'd shown him so far.

"Gwen," he murmured, sounding almost relieved. "It is you. I wasn't sure when I spotted you on the street, but I was hoping."

He gave her a crooked grin and then glanced past her, into the apartment. "Aren't you going to ask me in?"

"Actually," she drawled, groping behind her on the counter for her purse, "I was just on my way out."

"Great, I'll go with you."

That stopped her cold, causing her belly to lurch in panic. Darn it. She'd blurted the first thing that came to mind, never thinking he might want to go along…to wherever it was she now had to go.

"Um…"

"Come on," he cajoled. "I'll even drive."

One shoulder resting against the doorjamb, he was entirely too charming to deny.

She dropped her head and sighed. "All right, let me just take care of one thing first."

Before he could stop her, she slammed the door closed, then slung the strap of her purse over her shoulder on the way to the phone.

Apologizing profusely, she made up a story about a personal emergency and begged her supervisor at the library for the afternoon off, all the while gathering the bread, lettuce, mayonnaise and lunch meat she'd gotten out earlier and returning them to the refrigerator.

Marilyn, thank goodness, was completely understanding, but Gwen wondered how many more times she could call out with these flimsy excuses before someone either became suspicious or she lost her job.

After hanging up, she pulled the door open again and slipped into the hall, locking the apartment behind her.

"So." Ethan pushed away from the wall and rubbed his hands together in eagerness, still smiling. "You ready?"

Gwen nodded, walking ahead of him.

Seemingly unoffended, he matched his stride to hers. "Is there some reason you don't want me inside your apartment?" he asked in a casual tone.

His question brought her up short. She'd been hoping he wouldn't notice all her stealthy movements, but, of course, the man was too observant by half.

"No, not at all."

She cast a wary glance over her shoulder as they reached the stairwell, trying to read the expression on his face. The only thing she saw there was a degree of friendly curiosity and the strong, masculine features that encouraged the tiny butterflies low in her belly to start doing handsprings.

"It's just that…my place is a mess, and I was embarrassed for you to see it that way."

Yes, that sounded good. A plausible excuse.

"Maybe you can come in some other time, after I've had a chance to clean up." With any luck, that time would never come. Because if he ever discovered the kind of person she really was, she doubted he'd stick around long enough to get into her apartment.

"Okay," he responded with a shrug.

They started down the steps and almost reached the lobby before he spoke again.

"Where are we going, anyway?"

Good question. She hadn't really given it that much thought when she lied about being on her way out. Then her stomach growled, reminding her that she hadn't eaten anything since a slice of toast that morning.

"I thought I'd go out for lunch," she told him.

"Great." He slammed a hip against the metal bar of one of the plate-glass doors that fronted her building, holding it open until she stepped through. "Just tell me where. My car is parked nearby."

He pointed toward a long line of vehicles at the curb, and she followed him. And followed him. And followed him.

Several blocks later he stopped beside a silver Lexus, clicked the button on his keychain for the locks to click open, then leaned over to open the passenger side door. She paused before getting in, gazing in the direction of her apartment building *way* down the street.

"I know," he said, reading her mind, his high cheek-bones flushing slightly in embarrassment. "But it's a busy time of day and I was lucky to find this spot."

She was inside, fastening her seat belt, when a question occurred to her. As soon as he slid in next to her, she took a deep breath and asked.

"Ethan, I know this might sound strange, but how did you find me? I mean, that night we were to-gether…" Her voice broke and she stopped to clear her throat. "I know I didn't tell you where I lived."

Once again, a light brush of color swept across his features. "Yeah, well. You'll think I'm crazy, but I thought I saw you coming out of the library, so I pulled over and followed you."

"You followed me." She repeated his words, blinking like an owl in astonishment.

"I told you you'd think I was crazy, but I'm not a stalker, I swear," he said, flashing her a smile she thought was supposed to be reassuring. Then he turned his attention to the road and eased his car into the flow of traffic.

"The truth is, I wasn't sure it was you at first. You changed your hair."

Automatically Gwen lifted a hand to her shoulder-length curls. Was that *all* he'd noticed about her?

Now that she knew he'd seen her walking home on her lunch break, she realized he'd also seen her in the long, floral sundress and practical shoes she'd worn to work. Her mad rush to change into something he'd find more attractive probably hadn't even been necessary.

Except that she still didn't want him to know what kind of person she really was. Plain, boring, inhibited…all the things she'd fought so hard not to be the night they were together.

Her mind raced to come up with an excuse, some logical reason she'd been dressed that way. And then she realized he hadn't asked.

She felt a whisper of relief, followed by a grim determination that if he did ask about her earlier outfit, she'd simply lie. She could tell him she'd been to visit her parents in Virginia, and that they didn't approve of her normal, more outrageous clothing. And with the local library so close to her apartment building, it was only natural that she would borrow or need to return an occasional book.

"I like it," he murmured suddenly, drawing her away from the details of her made-up life.

"Excuse me?"

"Your hair. I liked it when it had more red in it, but this is nice, too. Soft and touchable." He reached out to do just that, rubbing the ends of a single curl between his thumb and fingers.

Gwen wasn't sure how it happened, since he wasn't actually touching her, but a bolt of electricity shot straight from the top of her scalp to the soles of her feet. Every inch of flesh in between tingled with awareness. Not to mention a few deep, dark places she hadn't known existed until she met this man.

When he released the lock of hair and returned his hand to the steering wheel, she immediately felt bereft.

"Why did you change it?" he wanted to know.

"I was just…in the mood for something different," she responded, thinking how much of an understatement that was. She'd been in the mood to change her life, her hair being only a small part of the major overhaul.

Unfortunately, she hadn't yet had the courage to introduce her new self to her friends at work. Which only proved what a coward she really was. No amount of makeup or shopping for new clothes could change that.

"So where are we going for lunch?"

She hadn't thought that far ahead, and all the places that popped into her head seemed too cheap or casual for someone with Ethan's style and tastes.

Shrugging a shoulder, she said, "I hadn't really decided yet."

"In that case, I'll take you to one of my favorites. They have great food and fairly private tables. It will give us a chance to get to know each other better."

Gwen swallowed and desperately longed to start today over again. If she'd known how much trouble she would be getting into, there wasn't a single thing she'd do the same.

But because she'd gone home in the middle of the afternoon instead of taking a bag lunch with her to work…because she'd opened her door when Ethan knocked…because she'd made up that stupid story about planning to go out for lunch …she would now have to make small talk with the one person in the world she didn't want knowing her any better.

It was almost enough to make her wish she'd remained a virgin.

Five

He took her to Martin's Tavern. Just about every white-collar worker in the Georgetown area ate there during lunchtime, so it was still pretty crowded. But the food was great, and in about ten minutes, the crowd would start to dwindle.

When the hostess offered to seat them, Ethan asked for something in the back where he and Gwen could hopefully have a bit of privacy. They followed the woman to a burgundy vinyl booth. A light green bar lamp hung overhead, casting a muted glow over the scarred, dark wood tabletop. Even in the middle of the day, the natural sunlight streaming through the front windows wasn't strong enough to completely illuminate the back of the tavern.

A few minutes later, a college-age waiter came to take their drink orders, then left them alone again to study the menus.

Ethan glanced surreptitiously at the woman sitting across from him, her nose buried in the laminated list of lunch choices. He couldn't believe it was really Gwen. That he'd found her on his own, out of the blue, when he'd been about twelve hours from hiring a detective to track her down.

She looked different from the way she had that night at his apartment, but in a good way. Her hair was styled in a more carefree fashion, without half a can of hairspray holding it in place. Her clothes looked more comfortable, too. Better suited to her personality—at least, the personality he'd seen glimpses of. Though he had to admit, he had a soft spot for the little black dress she'd worn on her birthday.

Thankfully, her eyes hadn't changed at all. They were the same melted milk chocolate he remembered. And her smile still had that girlish quality he'd noticed during their night together, even though she hadn't had much cause to use it since he surprised her at her apartment door not twenty minutes ago.

He wasn't sure there was a logical reason for his high spirits, but just seeing her again made the blood sing in his veins.

What the hell was wrong with him?

And what was so special about this woman, that she seemed to invade his every brain cell?

She wasn't his usual type, yet her face popped into his head the minute he woke up in the morning and was the last thing he saw before falling asleep at night. He spent his days wondering where she was, *who* she was, what she was doing, and if he'd ever see her again.

Now she sat across from him, her peach-tipped fingers drumming absently on the table while she perused her menu, and he couldn't think of a darn thing to say. Not a single question that had been burning in his gut for days. He found himself just being grateful he'd stumbled upon her and that she'd agreed to have lunch with him.

The waiter returned then, and they each ordered a sandwich platter. After he left, they sipped iced tea and made insignificant small talk until their meals arrived.

"You're right, the food is delicious," Gwen said, after taking a bite of her carved turkey on whole wheat. A drop of mustard dotted the corner of her mouth, and she lifted the cloth napkin from her lap to wipe it away.

He eyed his own club sandwich and the side of potato chips that had come with it. "I'm glad you like it."

Long seconds ticked by while they ate, until Ethan couldn't stand it anymore. He'd never before been shy, so he didn't see why the hell he should start now.

"Look, Gwen," he finally muttered. "There's something I've been wondering, so I'm just going to come out and ask."

He had the satisfaction of seeing her blanch as she struggled to swallow the chip she'd been chewing.

"The night we were together, why did you leave the next morning without saying anything? I mean, I got your note, but you didn't need to run off like that."

And why, oh, *why,* for the first time in his life, did it bother him so damn much?

She opened her mouth to speak, but the chip apparently went down the wrong way and she coughed instead. After taking a rather long sip of her iced tea, she inhaled deeply and raised her eyes to his.

He expected her to look away, but she surprised him by holding his gaze.

"I guess I was feeling uncomfortable, and thought it would be easier for both of us if I left before you woke up. You might not believe this, but I don't make a habit of going home—or to bed—with men I barely know."

At that she looked away, and he watched one perfectly rounded nail, painted a pale peach, draw circle eights on the tabletop.

"I do believe you. In fact, that's something else I've been wondering—why you would go home with me, a complete stranger, and ask me to make love to you."

He paused to take a sip of his own cold drink, letting his words sink in before adding what he knew to be true but wasn't sure she wanted known. "That's not something I'd have expected from a woman who had never been with a man before."

If she'd appeared uncomfortable before, she looked positively nauseated now. Her fidgeting finger stilled on the dark wood surface a moment, before she clasped her hands tightly in her lap.

"How did you know?" she asked in a strained whisper.

"There were some telltale signs," he answered frankly. "You seemed a little nervous at first, and it took you a while to warm up. You were also tighter than normal, and I felt the resistance when I got all the way inside you."

Color ranging from light pink to bright scarlet crept up her neck to stain her cheeks. Regret at his cavalier attitude tugged at his gut and he reached out to pat her arm.

"I'm sorry, I didn't mean to embarrass you. And you shouldn't be. Being a virgin is nothing to be ashamed of."

"I'm not ashamed," she responded.

The slope of her shoulders and lowering of her lashes told him differently, but he didn't press the issue.

"Good," he said simply. "Actually, it's kind of refreshing. Owning a nightclub, I come in contact with a number of women on a daily basis. I've even gone to bed with some of them," he told her matter-of-factly. "But I can't remember the last time I was a woman's first lover—if ever."

She glanced up, her Bambi-brown eyes anxious and wary. Ethan offered a small smile in an attempt to put her more at ease.

"Can you at least tell me why?" he asked.

"Why?"

"Why you picked me. Of all the men in George-town, and all the places you could have gone that night, why did you end up at The Hot Spot and with me?"

"Would you believe you were a birthday present to myself?" she asked softly.

He sat staring at her for a long minute, trying to absorb what she'd just told him. He'd known that night was her birthday, but hadn't realized he'd been her biggest present.

Should he feel used or flattered? He wasn't sure at this point. And he supposed he couldn't be too upset, considering the size of the gift she'd given him that night.

"Are you angry with me?"

He automatically shook his head. He was a lot of things, but angry wasn't one of them. "No, I'm not angry."

He wasn't, though he'd have been hard-pressed to describe his current emotions. A dozen proverbs floated through his head, making him want to chuckle. What Comes Around Goes Around.... The

Shoe Was on the Other Foot…. A Taste of His Own Medicine….

Yep, he'd had a good, long run of living a high, care-free life, and now this woman had come along to shake things up and make him doubt his whole existence.

Instead of making him feel better, however, her admission only raised more questions.

"Do you mind if I ask which birthday this was?" She didn't look a day over twenty-five, but he wasn't exactly an expert at pegging people's ages.

"Or maybe I should ask how it is that a beautiful, captivating young woman such as you manages to avoid going to bed with a man for so long, regard-less of how old you are. I would have expected you to lose your virginity in high school, maybe in the backseat of an old, beat-up car with the captain of the football team. Or on prom night with some frat boy you convinced your parents to let you date, even though you were still too young."

Gwen nearly choked at Ethan's so-very-wrong assumptions. It was hard enough to sit here, listen-ing to him talk about what *they'd* done that night and trying to form answers to questions she'd hoped never to be asked. But to hear him discuss her vir-ginity as though it was as common a topic as the weather… Or for him to think she might have been popular enough in high school to even *have* a boy-friend, let alone go all the way with one…

The truth was the captain of the football team hadn't known she existed, never mind being interested enough to try to get her into the backseat of his car. And there had been no prom for her. Only a night spent at home, reading and studying, as usual.

Most of her graduating class probably wouldn't even recognize her name. If pressed, maybe, *possibly*, a small portion might recall a thin, gangly girl with stringy brown hair and big, owlish glasses wandering the hall. But otherwise, they'd all been too preoccupied with their own social lives to notice her.

She was nothing like the person he obviously believed her to be, and no amount of new clothes or salon hairstyles was going to change that.

The question was, how did she tell him that, without ruining the one fun, exciting memory she had by admitting he'd gone to bed with a fraud?

"I grew up in a rather sheltered environment," she told him, which wasn't far from the truth. "And after that, I guess I was just…picky."

"Picky," he repeated, rolling the word around in his mouth as if he was trying to discern its meaning. "And yet you walked into my club one Friday night and decided to go home with the first man you met."

She swallowed the lump of dread squeezing her esophagus and threatening to cut off her air. "Technically, you were the second man I met."

He raised a brow, and she thought she saw one corner of his mouth tick with suppressed humor.

"I guess you're right. And you should be glad you didn't wind up leaving with that first guy. He's at The Hot Spot every night, it seems, hitting on unsuspecting women."

"And you aren't?"

His smile revealed sparkling white teeth. "I own the place. I have to be there. Besides, women hit on me more than I hit on them."

She didn't doubt that for a minute. Ethan was by far the most handsome man she'd seen at the club the night of her birthday.

Even now, she didn't think there was another man in the restaurant half as attractive as he was. Aside from his dark good looks, there was an aura about him that begged for attention. The way he carried himself and his obvious self-confidence drew people—especially women—to him like moths to a flame.

"But that still doesn't answer my question, does it?" he continued. "Why me? Why, after twenty-odd years, did you wake up and decide to get horizontal with a complete stranger?"

Tamping down a trickle of panic, she shifted in her chair, stiffening her spine. She didn't correct him on the "twenty-odd years" comment, either.

"Does it matter?" she retorted, a bit of snap to her

tone. "Do you grill other women you sleep with this way, or am I getting some sort of special treatment?"

Several seconds ticked by, while he stared at her and she stared back. Her heart was hammering a mile a minute, and a tiny voice in her head prayed he wouldn't be offended or annoyed enough to get up and walk out on her.

She liked him so much, but she was making a royal mess of seeing him again. All because she was too afraid of blatant rejection to tell him she normally wore cotton instead of lycra, brushed her hair rather than teased it and had never been to a nightclub in her life before the evening they'd met.

"You're right," he said finally. "It's none of my business who you sleep with or why…whether it's your first time or your four hundredth." With a wry twist to his lips, he added, "Though I am kind of glad I wasn't your four hundredth."

Four hundred. Right. She hadn't even begun to contemplate lover number two yet.

"How many women have you been with?" The query slipped out before she could stop it. "I'm sorry," she quickly apologized. "I shouldn't have asked that."

"Hey, it's no worse than what I was asking you."

He sat silently for a moment, absently stirring the long spoon in his glass of tea, making the ice cubes tinkle in reply.

"I guess the best thing for me to do here is come clean and say I honestly don't have a clue. That doesn't sound good or cast me in the best light, but it's the truth."

"That many, huh?"

He shrugged. "I own a popular nightclub where beautiful, single women come looking for a good time, and I never claimed to be a monk. The funny thing is…" He paused a beat to drum his fingers on the tabletop, his eyes growing smoky and serious as he held her attention. "I was completely faithful to my wife. From the time we started dating, I never even looked at another woman."

Gwen's mouth fell open, and she knew her eyes must be as wide as saucers. Of all the things she might have expected to hear from this man, that he'd had a wife wasn't one of them. She'd have been less flabbergasted to hear he wore ladies' underwear or sang in an all-male revue.

"You were married?"

"For almost five years," he said with a nod.

"What happened?"

"She married me for my money," he answered succinctly and with a clear note of bitterness. "Or rather, for my family's money. Of course, I didn't know that until I struck out on my own to open The Hot Spot. When things got tight, and without my parents' money to keep her in the lifestyle to which she'd become accustomed, she divorced me and took off for greener pastures."

Ethan lifted the tea to his mouth for a sip before continuing. "Her loss, though. The club is a huge success and now I'm rolling in it. So much so that I've been looking into buying property at a second location."

"Congratulations. You should be very proud of yourself, doing it all on your own, even though your parents were wealthy."

"Thank you. I am."

He was also still hurting from his ex-wife's betrayal. She could hear it in his voice and see it in the closed expression on his face.

"It probably isn't my place to say this, but you should also be glad your wife left you when she did. It would have been terrible to be married to someone who cared only for your money and not know it until it was too late."

He blinked as he considered her words. "I never thought of it that way," he murmured quietly. "I guess you're right."

Gwen glanced down, toying with the leftover slivers of potato chips on her plate.

"What about you?" he asked, causing her to lift her head. "Doesn't my money and success impress you?"

"Of course," she responded immediately. "I think it's wonderful that you had a dream and went after it, even if it meant leaving the financial security your family could have provided."

His gaze narrowed. "I meant *my* money. Doesn't it make you want to flirt with me, latch on to me, see if you can squeeze a few expensive pieces of jewelry, or maybe a sports car, out of me before we go our separate ways?"

Her lips tightened in a moue of annoyance. "I don't know what kind of women you're used to hanging around with at that club of yours, but I'm not after your money. You came to *my* apartment today, remember? If you hadn't, we probably never would have seen each other again. I make a fine income on my own and don't need anyone else to support me. I certainly don't need a man to buy me things. If there's something I want, I'll either buy it myself or do without."

Time ticked by after her fervent speech, with nothing but the clink of silverware and the muted voices of other diners to fill the taut silence. And then Ethan threw his head back and laughed.

At first she thought she might have sent him over the edge, but the longer he chuckled, the more she realized he was genuinely amused.

Heads turned toward them, people wondering what was so funny. But instead of feeling uncomfortable under their close scrutiny, she was simply glad Ethan appeared to be enjoying himself.

It couldn't be easy coming to terms with the fact that the person you loved and had married—the woman you thought loved you in return—was really only interested in your family's fortune and what it could buy.

"You know what, Gwen?" he managed, once he'd caught his breath.

"What?"

"I'm glad you picked me as your birthday present."

A ripple of delight—followed closely by pure, unadulterated desire—washed over her, raising the hairs on her arms and making her knees clench together.

She was glad, too, but would never admit to him how much.

Their waiter returned then, to take away their empty plates and offer dessert. Gwen passed, but Ethan ordered a slice of key lime pie and a cup of coffee to wash it down.

"Will you do me a favor?" he asked while they waited for his order to arrive.

She studied him warily, not sure she wanted to agree to anything until she'd heard him out. "What kind of favor?"

"I'm having a small dinner party at the club next week and I'd like you to come."

"I don't think that's a good idea," she replied, after thinking it over for a couple of seconds.

"Please. You won't feel out of place, I promise. My best friend and his wife are coming over, and if you aren't there to act as a buffer, I'll be alone with them. I love them like family, but ever since they got married, every time we get together Lucy tries to reform me. Before the wine has even been uncorked, she'll start lecturing me on the error of my ways, and naming every decent, single female she knows who might make a good wife. If I have a date with me, though, Lucy will hold her tongue and give me a much-needed break from her efforts to see me settled down."

"Let me guess. She'll leave *you* alone, but get it into her head that *I* might be just the girl to 'reform' you, and spend the entire evening quizzing me on my methods."

Ethan grinned widely at her and dug into his pie as soon as the waiter placed it in front of him.

"I don't doubt for a minute that she'll try. Lucy can be a bulldog about these things. But I'll protect you and keep her from badgering you too much. If I make it clear you're just another flavor of the month and elicit Peter's help, we should be able to keep her from going overboard."

"Is that what I am, then," she asked softly, "the flavor of the month?"

He swallowed his last bite of pie and carefully set the fork across the plate, finally meeting her gaze. "No, actually. I'd like to think we're becoming friends."

With a sigh, Gwen leaned back in the booth and shook her head. Until he showed up at her apartment door this afternoon, he'd been a one-night stand, and now he believed they were becoming friends.

"I know I'm likely to regret this," she said, "but what time will you be picking me up?"

Six

Ethan stood over the bench press, spotting Peter as he lifted a fifty-pound weight. Arms crossed over his chest, Ethan glared down at his supposed best friend.

"I can't believe you're giving me a hard time about this. What's the big deal about loading Lucy into the car and bringing her over to the club?"

"Hey, watch it. You're making my wife sound like a head of cattle. She isn't that big yet, and besides, I think she looks cute."

"I didn't mean it that way," Ethan nearly growled in frustration. "Of course she's cute. She looks like she swallowed a basketball, but I guess that's better than looking like she swallowed a Buick."

With a grunt, Peter lifted the barbell a final time, and Ethan helped him fit it into place.

"Here's what I don't get," Peter said, slightly out of breath as he sat up and began using one of the towels the gym provided to wipe a layer of sweat from his face and neck. "You scoff at Lucy's pregnancy, and the fact that we're deliriously happy together, yet you come to me and ask this favor to impress a woman. A woman who—if I didn't know better—has got you considering the marriage and family route yourself."

"I've been married," Ethan replied tersely. "It didn't work out."

"That's because Susan was a tramp and a gold digger. You're older and wiser now." His friend gave him a sardonic look. "Or so one would hope, though you couldn't prove it by those empty-headed bimbos you take home."

Ethan bit the inside of his lip and clenched his fists beneath his crossed arms. If Peter weren't his best friend, he'd have probably popped him one already.

"What's your point?"

"My point is, you've never asked Lucy and me to dinner before to meet one of your lady friends. In fact, other than flaunting your one-night stands when you feel like playing the playboy bachelor to the hilt, you rarely talk about the women you're interested in at all."

Peter narrowed his eyes. "Now, suddenly, it's become imperative that you set up this dinner party at
The Hot Spot, and that Lucy and I are both there.
Why? Do you like this girl that much? Or are you trying to shake her loose and need my wife to grill her
like a nice, juicy steak?"

Peter grinned and Ethan couldn't help but smile
in return. "I'm not trying to shake this one loose. And
I want you to keep Lucy on a short leash, if you can."

"Hey, she's got a mind of her own. I'm just along
for the ride," he said with a shrug. "So I guess that
means you like this one, huh?"

A stab of fear lanced Ethan's belly. No, he wasn't
ready to say that, at least the scene that Peter meant,
but there was something about Gwen that kept her in
the forefront of his mind.

He thought of the way she'd looked when he'd
dropped her off after their lunch yesterday. He'd let
her out at the curb, but only after she'd made a point
of telling him about a dozen times that he didn't need
to bother finding a parking space or walking her to
her apartment.

He'd taken the hint, but kept his car idling and
watched her walk away. It would have taken a saint
not to admire the snug fit of her snow-white jeans or
the gentle sway of her shapely bottom—and he was
far from being a saint.

He'd also noticed how she kept glancing over her

shoulder, as if she expected him not to be there. As if he'd have pulled away as soon as the car door slammed behind her.

Please. If she'd stood in front of her building for an hour, staring up at the sky, he'd have flipped on his blinkers and pretended to be having engine trouble until the cops came to chase him away.

"I wouldn't go that far," he told his friend, despite the thoughts rolling through his head. "But I would like to get to know her a little better, which is why I need you and Lucy to come to this dinner Wednesday night. She'll like you two, and I know you'll like her. You won't have to worry about a thing. I've already called the caterer, so everything's set."

Peter pushed to his feet and headed for the shower. "I'll talk to Lucy about it, but I'm not making any promises."

"Great," Ethan offered, close on his buddy's heels. "Thanks. Tell Lucy I'd really appreciate it. And I'll owe her one, if she agrees. Maybe I can babysit her cat again the next time you two go out of town."

"Maybe you can babysit the baby."

Ethan made a face, imagining himself at the mercy of a squalling infant. Not to mention the bottles of formula, dirty diapers and shoulders covered in baby puke.

Swallowing hard, he forced his mouth to move. "If that's what it takes, I guess I'll have to. Provided you trust me to take care of your kid."

Peter halted in midstride and he turned to Ethan, his brows drawn together as he considered what he'd said. "Yeah, you're right. I may have to give it a bit more thought, but I'm sure we'll come up with something. Oh, and if we do make it Wednesday night, be sure to have plenty of beets on hand."

"Beets?"

"Yeah, it's Lucy's latest craving. If you don't have some around, she's likely to bite your hand off."

"Beets." Ethan gave a heartfelt sigh and scrubbed a hand over his face. This was all getting way too complicated. "All right, got it. I'll tell the caterer to bring a bushel of beets."

Gwen succeeded in putting her lunch and upcoming dinner with Ethan completely out of her mind…right up until Wednesday morning, when she opened her closet and realized she once again had nothing to wear.

Or at least nothing she thought would be appropriate for spending an evening at his nightclub, with his friends, who were likely far more sophisticated than she was.

What were his friends like, she wondered?

Were they young, flashy, fun?

Would she be seated next to a blond bombshell with silicone boobs, or some greasy faux movie producer who would slyly invite her to an audition on his casting couch when no one was looking?

All right, so that wasn't entirely fair. She was projecting. Not to mention stereotyping people she hadn't even met yet.

For all she knew, Ethan's friends might be the most pleasant folks she'd ever meet.

Ethan certainly wasn't what she would have expected if someone had told her about the nightclub owner before she'd actually met him. He was nice and kind of…sweet.

He'd tracked her down after she'd thought their short-lived acquaintance long over.

He'd taken her to lunch, to his favorite restaurant, which was apparently *the* place for everyone from secretaries to visiting diplomats to spend their lunch breaks. And he'd refused to let her pay—not even the tip.

Then, to top it all off, he'd asked her to dinner, to meet some of his friends.

So maybe things weren't always what they seemed. She was a prime example of that. She was nothing like what she seemed—at least, not when she was around Ethan.

But she couldn't tell him the truth, couldn't let him see the real Gwen Thomas, because then he might not be interested in her or want to spend time with her anymore. And even though she knew their relationship would end, she couldn't quite bear for it to end *yet*.

She liked being with him, liked thinking about being with him again. And she thrilled at the knowledge that she'd been in his bed, knew him intimately, even if she didn't know him very well beyond the physical.

But she hoped to.

Which meant she needed to get back to that boutique and find something appropriate for tonight.

She went straight to the shop after work and spent a good two hours trying on cocktail dresses of all colors and designs. When she came out of the dressing room for what felt like the hundredth time, the owner of the boutique gasped and clapped her hands together in delight.

"Oh, honey, that's the one."

Latifa, the tall black woman with fuchsia highlights in her hair who had helped her to choose her birthday ensemble and some of the other new items in her closet, stepped forward and began brushing her hands over Gwen's body, checking the seams and the fit of the dress.

It was a form-fitting, strapless sheath in fire-engine red that fell slightly north of midthigh. Stretchy filigree lace covered the satin body of the dress, which came with a matching, short-waisted, long-sleeve jacket.

Standing in front of the boutique's angled, full-length mirrors, Gwen thought she looked as much like a catalog model as she ever would. She couldn't remember ever owning anything so feminine and beautiful and sort of…sireny, if that was even a word.

The price tag dangling from the sleeve nearly sent her into cardiac arrest, but she took a deep breath and tried to mentally calculate whether or not she could afford it.

Maybe if she picked up a few extra hours at the library and packed peanut butter and jelly sandwiches for her lunch for a while…

"Are you sure the color is right for a dinner party?" Gwen asked.

"Oh, yeah. Not for everyone, or under certain circumstances, but on you it looks like a million bucks. You could wear that dress to church on Sunday and no one would say a word."

Latifa gave a little chuckle and stepped away, hands on her hips. "The men might be thinking thoughts that would send them straight to hell, but that wouldn't be your problem."

The color did seem to bring out her eyes and the deeper shades in her hair. Not to mention that the dress's snug fit displayed hills and valleys she hadn't seen since she dropped by Ethan's nightclub the first time. She actually appeared to have decent-size breasts for a change, and looked like more than a popsicle stick in ladies' footwear.

A part of her thought the outfit might be too much. But then, wasn't that what she was going for? She'd been *too much* the night of her birthday and landed Ethan without even trying.

Since then, she'd pulled back from that blatant, highly sensual side of herself, but he didn't know that. The woman in the high-cut red dress staring back at her from three different angles was exactly who he would be expecting to greet him when he picked her up this evening.

And if she switched to peanut butter and jelly sandwiches for lunch and dinner both, and didn't buy any more clothes for a while…she might be able to swing it.

"I hope you're right about this," she said, her stomach knotted with anxiety.

"Oh, honey, I'm right. Once he sees you, that man of yours is going to have a hard time keeping his tongue in his mouth."

"He's not 'my man,'" Gwen corrected, letting her gaze fall to the floor.

"Not yet, you mean. But you come back tomorrow and tell Miss Latifa if that hasn't changed."

The woman's smile was contagious, and she seemed so sure *this* was the dress.

"Okay," Gwen agreed, "but I'm also going to need shoes and accessories." And, like the Cowardly Lion, she needed some courage to get through the evening unscathed.

"You do take credit cards, right?"

Gwen was dressed and ready to go by the time Ethan knocked on her door that evening. She hadn't wanted to risk needing more time, in which case she'd be forced to invite him inside, where he might feel the need to peek around while she finished getting prepared.

In addition to the red dress that made her feel like a movie star, she was wearing seamed stockings and red satin pumps. Her ears were adorned with gold hoops, and gold chains sparkled at her neck and wrist. Her hair was hanging loose around her shoulders, the sides held up with two tiny, almost invisible combs.

The boutique owner had also talked her into purchasing a small, sequined handbag to round out the ensemble. Gwen had stuffed a compact, lipstick and the key to her apartment inside, then waited in the kitchen, her heart pounding in anticipation, for Ethan to arrive.

Even though she'd been expecting him, had been listening for his footsteps in the hall for more than half an hour, she still jumped at that first loud, confident rap on the door.

Taking a deep breath, she swallowed and bounced

a few times on the balls of her feet, ordering her nerves to stop skittering around like live electrical wires. When she felt more in control of her emotions, she twisted the knob and yanked open the door.

Once again his mere presence punched her in the solar plexus, knocking the air from her lungs for a brief second.

He stood in the hallway, feet apart, one hand resting on the doorjamb, the other tucked into the pocket of his tailored charcoal slacks. The smile on his face was sexy and charming, the gleam in his eyes flirty and playful. His jacket matched his pants, but the silk shirt beneath was a vibrant emerald green that screamed hot and hip.

For tonight, at least, she was hot and hip, too—or pretending to be—so she refused to be intimidated. Outwardly, anyway.

Grinning with an enthusiasm she didn't quite feel, she slipped the gold chain strap of her purse over her shoulder and closed the door behind her with a click.

"Hi," she said.

"Hi," he returned distractedly, his gaze traveling up and down her body. "Wow. I hope you don't take offense at that," he quickly added, holding his palms up in a defenseless gesture, "but it's the best I can do with so little blood pumping to my brain. *Wow.*"

Her skin flushed with warmth at his blatant admission, and her eyes darted to the ground.

"You look amazing. And you can believe me when

I say that, because I've seen *a lot* of fashionable women." One corner of his mouth hitched higher, and he gave her a slow, sexy wink. "A side effect of owning a nightclub, you know. But that just makes me more of an authority on the subject, and I can honestly say you look *hot* tonight."

His persistence made her chuckle even as she blushed. "Thank you. I guess. You look very nice yourself."

"Thanks." He tugged at the edges of his jacket and straightened the collar of his shirt. "Are you ready to go?"

She jiggled the doorknob to her apartment one more time to be sure it was locked and then turned to face him again. "Ready."

He took her hand, linking his fingers with hers as they walked down the hall. "Thanks for letting me pick you up early. I didn't want you to have to take a cab, but I also thought I should be there when Peter and Lucy arrive."

Six o'clock might seem early to Ethan, but normally she would have already eaten and climbed into bed with a good book. He'd explained, though, that they needed to eat and have everything cleared away by the time The Hot Spot opened its doors for business at 10:00 p.m.

"It's not a problem. I'm looking forward to meeting your friends."

"You'll like them," he said, letting her descend the stairs ahead of him, but not loosening his hold on her.

"I'm sure I will. Are they the only ones who will be there?"

He shoved the lobby door open with his hip and waited for her to pass before answering. "Yeah. I hope that's okay."

"Of course. I just thought that since you said it was a dinner party, there would be more people there."

"It's a small dinner party. Four is plenty for that, don't you think?"

She thought he was going to an awful lot of trouble for friends he'd apparently known for years, but she didn't say so. Instead she murmured, "I suppose. I don't throw many dinner parties myself."

"Really?"

He opened the passenger door of his silver Lexus and helped her inside, only then releasing her hand. After circling the front of the car, he slid behind the wheel and turned the key.

"I would have thought you spent plenty of time entertaining. You seem like a girl who enjoys having fun."

His comment robbed her of breath and sent an icy-cold wash of reality through her system.

He was right; she *seemed* like a girl who liked to have a good time because that was who she was supposed to be, at least around him. How could she have been so careless as to admit she didn't go out much—or have people in, either?

Stupid, stupid, stupid. She would have to be more careful from now on or he would figure out that she wasn't at all the type of person she was pretending to be.

Mind racing, she grasped for a plausible response, something he would easily accept.

"I do," she said as steadily as she could manage. "I just tend to go out for my fun rather than inviting it in."

"I've noticed that," he responded without missing a beat.

Did that mean he believed her?

He shot her a meaningful glance. "I've been to your apartment twice now and you have yet to invite me in."

She swallowed nervously. "Did you want to come in?" she asked, hoping the question would come across as daring.

"Sure. You've seen my apartment, it's only fair that I get to see yours."

Oh, Lord. She'd seen his apartment, all right, including the bedroom. Did he expect her to reciprocate?

Not that she would mind making love with him again. The very thought warmed her from the inside out and made her tingle in places only he had ever touched.

But that didn't change the fact that she couldn't invite him inside. If she did, then he would see that she lived like a mild-mannered librarian or, more aptly, a thirty-one-year-old spinster instead of a party girl.

"I'll think about it," she said coyly.

Ten minutes later they parked behind The Hot Spot, and Ethan led her inside through a rear entrance.

Without strobe lights and a crush of colorfully dressed bodies, the interior of the club looked nothing like Gwen remembered. The dark, gleaming floors glowed in spots from muted track lighting.

An oblong table covered with a pristine white cloth and set with crystal stemware sat in the middle of the dance floor. Two chairs were situated on each of the longest sides, and two tall ivory tapers burned in shining silver candle holders surrounded by large, full-bloomed red and white roses.

The entire arrangement was very romantic, and for a moment Gwen was surprised by this side of Ethan. She wouldn't have expected it, considering his playboy lifestyle after a painful divorce, but it was a nice discovery.

"This is lovely," she said, stopping a few feet away from the table.

Ethan came to a halt beside her, his wide palm resting on her left hip while his arm spanned the back of her waist.

"As much as I might like to, I'm afraid I can't take

the credit. I told the caterers what I wanted and they took care of the rest."

"In that case, you hired very competent caterers," she teased.

"Thank you."

Stepping forward, he lifted an uncorked bottle of wine from the table.

"Here," he said, filling a glass with the rich red liquid and handing it to her. "Have a seat and sip some wine while I make sure everything's running on schedule. I'll be right back."

He disappeared before she could protest, and she was left staring at the wide-open club space and the candles flickering on the tabletop. Lifting the glass to her lips, she took a small swallow, welcoming the soothing smoothness of the alcohol as it ran down her throat and warmed her belly.

Mmm. If she kept a full glass of this delicious wine in her hand all night, she might just make it through dinner without succumbing to a massive panic attack.

The front door of the club opened as Gwen took a second sip from her glass, allowing the noises from outdoors inside the otherwise quiet building for a few brief seconds. Then the door closed and only footsteps and muted voices could be heard.

Taking a deep breath, Gwen set her wine on the table and ran her hands down the front of her dress to make sure everything was in place before Ethan's friends appeared.

And she knew it must be them. For everyone else, The Hot Spot was closed. Even if it hadn't been, the party crowd wouldn't start showing up until much closer to midnight.

An attractive couple rounded the tall partition that separated the dance area from the bar and stopped, friendly smiles on their faces.

The woman was tall, with long, straight black hair. Her red lipstick suited her light complexion perfectly. She wore a calf-length dress in black, with large lavender tulips and greenery decorating the otherwise plain material. The spaghetti straps and half-moon neckline left her chest and shoulders bare, except for a thin gold chain bearing a small heart-shaped charm that sparkled with diamonds. Her shoes were sensible black pumps, the heels no higher than an inch. For safety reasons, Gwen suspected, given the noticeable bulge at her middle.

The man was equally tall, with sandy-blond hair, looking decidedly uncomfortable in his gray suit coat and diagonally striped tie.

Gwen knew she should say something, do something, but all she seemed capable of at the moment was wringing her hands together.

Thankfully, the other woman wasn't nearly as beset by nerves as Gwen was. She stepped forward, kindness glowing in her bright-blue eyes as she offered Gwen her hand.

"Hi, there. You must be Gwen. I'm Lucy, and this is my husband, Peter." Turning slightly, she pulled the man forward by his sleeve.

"Nice to meet you," he murmured, shaking her hand briefly.

"It's nice to meet you, too. Both of you."

Gwen glanced in the direction Ethan had gone, wondering how much longer he would be. "Ethan just went to check on dinner. He should be back any minute."

"Oh, don't worry about him," Lucy said, waving off her comment. "He'll show up eventually. In the meantime, let's sit down and get to know each other better."

Peter held out a chair for his wife, and probably would have done the same for Gwen if she hadn't already picked a seat on the other side of the table near her wine glass.

Instead of joining them, Peter took a step back, casually caressing Lucy's bare arm. "I think I'll go find Ethan. Will you two be all right out here while I'm gone?"

One corner of Lucy's mouth quirked upward in amusement. "I think we'll survive. But tell Ethan not to take long. I'm eating for two now, and the baby's famished."

As soon as Peter was out of earshot, Lucy leaned closer and said, "He's a little overprotective. Once in a while it gets annoying, but for the most part, I let him go. It makes him feel more involved to hover and bring me warm milk and cookies at 3:00 a.m."

"He obviously cares about you a great deal." Gwen didn't know what else to say, and covered her insecurities by sipping at her wine.

"He does," Lucy replied, her cheeks rosy with happiness. She poured herself a glass of ice water from the pitcher on the table and took a drink before continuing.

"But enough about Peter and me. What I really want to know is how hot and heavy things are between you and Ethan."

Seven

Gwen's lungs seized in her chest and she fought to swallow her last mouthful of wine before it shot out of her nose.

"I've been champing at the bit for details ever since Peter told me Ethan had invited us to dinner to meet his newest lady friend." Lucy tucked a strand of ebony hair behind her ear, oblivious to Gwen's ongoing panic attack.

When Gwen could breathe again—at least enough to keep from passing out—she coughed delicately into her linen napkin and said, "There's nothing to tell. I'm not Ethan's lady friend," she insisted, "and we are *not* hot and heavy."

Before the night she'd spent in Ethan's bed, she wasn't sure she'd even known the definition of "hot and heavy." She certainly knew what it meant now, but that night had been an isolated incident. The fact remained that they were not currently hot and heavy.

Lucy rolled her eyes and absently rubbed her hands in circles over the mound of her belly. "Oh, come on. To my knowledge, he's never done anything like this before. In fact, I don't think he's ever bothered to introduce us to any other woman he's dated—at the very least to Peter, who's his best friend. And I use the term *woman* loosely, by the way, given what I've gleaned about some of them."

Gwen cringed, realizing that she could be one of those women Lucy was talking about. After all, Ethan had taken her home with him and made love to her the first night they'd met…which was exactly what she'd been looking for at the time. So, in a way his playboy lifestyle had worked to her benefit.

And even if it hadn't, it didn't matter. Ethan's habits—sexual or otherwise—were none of her business.

Maybe if she and Ethan were involved, she would be concerned about how many women he slept with, and whether or not he was being faithful. But sadly, she was well aware that a man like Ethan could never be seriously interested in a woman like her.

She wasn't sure what his tracking her down at home or inviting her to dinner at the club this eve-

ning were all about, but she hadn't deluded herself
into thinking of either as signs that Ethan was trying
to build a relationship with her.

He was probably trying to impress his friends with
his ability to throw an intimate dinner party. Or perhaps her presence here tonight was simply his way
of getting them off his case about not having someone steady in his life.

The more she thought about it, the more she suspected her latter conclusion was the most likely reason for Ethan continuing his acquaintance with her.
If his friends and family were starting to badger him
about settling down, then she could certainly understand why he would want them to think he was sig-
nificantly involved with one woman.

Oh, no. Had she ruined it for him already by telling Lucy she wasn't his lady friend, that they weren't
"hot and heavy"?

Her mind raced, as she tried to recall exactly what
had been said and how the situation could be sal-
vaged. She didn't mind playing a part for Ethan.
Heck, she was already pretending to be someone she
wasn't. Why not expand her boundaries a bit by pretending to be both more worldly than she really was
and more involved with Ethan?

"What…um." She cleared her throat and toyed
with the stem of her wine glass instead of making
eye contact with the woman across the table from

her. "What did Ethan tell you and your husband about us?"

"Not much," Lucy said with a little huff. "Peter came home from the gym one day saying Ethan wanted us to come to the club for dinner, and that he was bringing a woman he wanted us to meet. Well, there was no way I could pass up an opportunity like that. The only female acquaintance of Ethan's I've ever met was a rather large-breasted peroxide blonde who answered the door in a see-through bra and pair of thong panties." She rolled her eyes in feigned horror. "Believe me, I never again made the mistake of dropping by his apartment without calling first."

Lucy lifted the water goblet to her lips, but offered a conspiratorial grin before drinking. "I suffered a nasty case of hysterical blindness for a week afterward. We decent, upstanding women shouldn't be assaulted with bimbos like that too often. It seriously skews our delicate sensibilities."

Gwen chuckled at Lucy's colorful storytelling before she could stop herself.

"You don't even know me," she felt the need to point out. "What makes you think I'm not one of Ethan's bubble-brained bimbos, too?"

"For one thing, you're a brunette, which means you haven't been frying brain cells with multiple bottles of bleach on a regular basis for years.

"For another, although your dress is sexy and a little daring—I love it, by the way, so you'll have to give me the name of the shop where you found it— it's not low enough for me to measure your cleavage or short enough for me to see your butt cheeks. But aside from your appearance, the mere fact that Ethan set up all of this—" she waved an arm to encompass the beautiful table setting, candles flickering at the motion "—and *asked* us to come meet you is enough to convince me you're special. He's never done that before because he usually doesn't *want* us to meet the kind of women he finds attractive.

"And last but not least, if you were one of Ethan's typical bimbo types, you wouldn't be sitting here holding an intelligent conversation with me. You'd be wherever Ethan is, hanging on his arm, snapping your gum and rubbing against him like a cat in heat. That's what they do, either in an effort to get him into bed more quickly or to wheedle expensive gifts out of him because they know he has money."

Gwen didn't know what to say, so she bit the inside of her lip and remained silent.

"Has he given you anything? A bracelet, necklace, some other pretty trinket?"

She wanted to shake her head and assure Lucy she wasn't using Ethan for his money or anything else, but if she was supposed to be his latest romantic interest, then it was plausible that Ethan might have given her a gift of some kind.

Still, she couldn't bring herself to lie.

"I don't think we've gotten to that point yet," she responded honestly. "We went out to lunch once, and he insisted on paying the bill, but we haven't been seeing each other long enough to exchange presents."

Lucy seemed to consider her answer for a moment. "I'm not sure what that means, to tell you the truth."

She sipped at her water and then worried the manicured nail of her index finger with her front teeth. "Let me ask you this. Has he mentioned Susan at all?"

"His ex-wife?" Gwen nodded. "Oh, yes, he told me about her."

"Interesting," Lucy said, drawing out the word. "What did he tell you?"

"Just that they'd been married for almost five years, and that she left him when he decided to open The Hot Spot without benefit of his parents' financial backing."

Gwen really didn't see the importance of that information, but Lucy apparently did. Her eyes widened and a small smile crept over her face.

"And what did you tell him?"

Gwen thought back to their discussion in Martin's Tavern. "I told him he was lucky to be rid of his ex, if all she cared about was his money."

"Do *you* care about his money?" Lucy asked.

Gwen's hackles went up. Why did everyone suddenly think she was out to find a man with a hefty bank account? Did she look needy, for some reason? Did she look as if she couldn't support herself? Granted, a librarian's salary wasn't exactly awe-inducing, but she was getting by just fine.

Taking a deep breath, she counted to ten before answering Lucy's question, for fear she might say something Ethan wouldn't appreciate her telling his best friend's wife.

"No, I don't. I don't need a man—or anyone else—to support me. Money, it seems, causes more problems than it solves. I think Ethan can attest to that."

Lucy studied her for several minutes. So long that Gwen actually began to squirm.

And then her expression lightened and she offered Gwen a friendly smile. "I don't want to get your hopes up, in case Ethan pulls a patently male move and gets cold feet," she murmured conspiratorially, "but you might just be the one, Gwen."

The one? What did Lucy mean by that?

But before she could press for more information, a door opened somewhere at the back of the club and footsteps sounded as Ethan and Peter approached. They laughed together easily and were both smiling when they came into the women's line of sight.

"There you are," Lucy teased, craning her neck backward to look at her husband. "We thought you'd run off to some fast-food joint and left us here to starve."

"Would I do that?" Peter asked, leaning forward to press an upside-down kiss on her lips.

"You might," she returned, "especially if you found out beets were being served."

He shuddered visibly and pulled out the empty chair beside her. "I've got news for you, sweetheart. As much as I'm coming to despise those wretched things, I told Ethan about your latest craving, so they *are* being served."

Looking amused, Ethan rounded the table and took a seat beside Gwen. "Peter and I just checked," he told Lucy. "There are enough warm beets back there to turn you purple with glee."

"Good, because I'm hungry enough to eat a horse and three sheep."

"So much for the delicacies of pregnancy, huh?" Ethan said in an aside to Gwen, leaning against her for a brief moment.

Heat branched out and spread through the rest of her body from just the small area of her arm, from shoulder to elbow, he touched with his own. She shifted quickly, wishing she didn't have this reaction to him every time they came in contact, but the sensation remained.

"Dinner will be a few more minutes," Ethan announced, pouring a glass of wine for Peter and himself.

"Oh, that's all right." Lucy grinned as she rested her elbows on the table, propping her chin on her steepled hands. "Gwen was just telling me about the two of you. How you've been going at it hot and heavy."

Gwen's mouth dropped open and worked like a fish struggling for oxygen out of water. She heard a gasping noise and realized it was coming from her.

Her gaze shot to Ethan. She expected to see his eyes narrowed, his mouth turned down in a frown. If she had been in his place, she would have been furious. Instead, his hazel eyes sparkled and his lips curved as he laughed.

"Is that so? I hope she didn't tell you what we did with the trampoline and chocolate sauce. That story is a little risqué, and I thought we should keep it to ourselves."

Lucy giggled like a schoolgirl while Peter's brows shot up, and Gwen saw her life flashing before her eyes.

Could this night get any worse?

First she'd had to dress up and pretend to be the same woman she'd been on her birthday, even though *that* woman was a figment of everyone's imagination.

Then Ethan's friend cornered her and made her think she was possibly supposed to be his fake girlfriend.

And now they were sitting around discussing bizarre sex acts that had never happened.

"Actually, I was teasing," Lucy said, "but if you'd like to regale us with the trampoline and chocolate sauce story, I'd love to hear it. Peter and I are always looking for new and creative techniques to try out in the bedroom."

"All right, all right," Peter cut in, throwing up his hands in front of his face as though to ward off any more sexual repartee. "Enough. I really don't need to hear any sex talk while I'm at dinner with my *pregnant* wife and another lovely young woman."

Gwen wanted to kiss him. And then she wanted to jump up and kiss the catering staff, who appeared a second later with four plates of leafy green salad and burgeoning shrimp cocktails to begin the meal.

After napkins had been shaken out and spread on laps and a bowl of beets brought for Lucy, they began to eat. Gwen even started to relax, thinking that the food would act as a distraction from what they'd been discussing only moments before.

She should have known she couldn't be so lucky.

"I'm sorry if we embarrassed you," Lucy said, breaking the silence and offering Gwen a comforting smile as she dabbed her lips. "We were just poking fun, the way good friends do, but we shouldn't have done it at your expense. You definitely haven't known us long enough to realize we didn't mean anything by it."

"That's all right," Gwen assured her. "I didn't take offense."

She had been embarrassed, but only because she was so unsure of herself and feeling so much out of her element. Sharing sexual experiences wasn't a typical pastime of the middle-aged librarians she worked with. They tended to gossip more about what books were hitting the bestseller lists.

"Still, let's change the subject," Lucy said.

Yes, please, Gwen thought desperately.

"We came here tonight to get to know you, not to make you squirm. So tell us a little about yourself, Gwen."

No! Please, no!

"Where do you work?"

Oh, God. What should she do?

She'd managed to avoid this conversation with Ethan until now, but it seemed she wasn't going to be able to avoid it any longer. Lucy had no idea what she was asking…or how fast Gwen had to mentally race to come up with an acceptable answer.

"I…um. I'm a buyer."

That was a real job, wasn't it? She blurted the words before she'd even realized her mouth was open, but she thought for sure she'd heard it discussed on television as an authentic occupation. Of course, that had been on a popular sitcom rather than some true-to-life documentary or news story, but still…

"Really? That's fascinating," Lucy replied, stabbing a forkful of lettuce on her salad plate.

"What is it you buy?" Peter asked.

Ethan, she noticed, remained curiously silent.

From the corner of her eye she saw that he was watching her intently.

She shouldn't be surprised. This was news to him, too, and he was probably just as eager as the others to hear the details of her so-called job as a "buyer." Of course, he couldn't ask any questions of his own or his friends might wonder why he didn't already know all this about her—his supposed current love interest.

"Clothes," she volunteered in response to Peter's inquiry. "I'm a fashion buyer for several high-end department stores and a few local boutiques."

Well, now she was downright stealing from that sitcom. But was it her fault she spent most of her evenings home alone, reading in front of the television? Or that the show had inadvertently supplied her with a job description that seemed to fit her alter ego to a T?

"Oooh, that explains your fabulous dress," Lucy gushed with enthusiasm.

Gwen glanced down at herself. "Yes," she lied. "I purchased a few of these for a small boutique downtown and ended up buying one for myself."

"Maybe we can go shopping together sometime. It will have to wait until after the little rugrat is born, though," Lucy added, patting her stomach, "because I don't plan to add any more nice clothes to my wardrobe until I can fit into them again."

Gwen smiled, relaxing a bit at having the conversation turn away from her. "When are you due?"

Lucy sighed. "Two more months. I can't wait."

She reached out to squeeze her husband's hand and they exchanged a look that made Gwen's heart lurch. The affection between them was obvious, but also almost painful to someone like Gwen who had never experienced anything even close to it.

"Peter is more nervous than he likes to let on," Lucy continued, "but I'm looking forward to motherhood, as well as getting my figure back."

"Nervous, hell," Peter grumbled around a mouthful of shrimp. "I'm petrified."

Lucy fussed over him for a few seconds, telling him he had nothing to worry about and that he would be a terrific father.

Ethan rolled his eyes. He'd seen and heard this exchange from his friends before, ad nauseam, and decided to tease them a little.

He leaned toward Gwen just as the main course was being brought out. "Sorry about this," he told her in a stage whisper. "Guess I should have invited someone other than these old, married folks to keep us company tonight."

"Hey," Peter snapped good-naturedly. "Wait until it's your turn. Someday while you're whining and fretting over the impending birth of your first child, I'll remind you of how unsympathetic you were with us. Not that there's a chance in hell of that happening anytime soon."

"You never know." Ethan waggled his brows and nuzzled the area just below Gwen's ear with his nose. "I have been throwing out a few feelers lately, trying to see who might be interested in bearing the next set of Banks descendents."

He didn't know why he'd said what he had. In his peripheral vision, he saw Peter and Lucy exchange curious glances, but he was more interested in Gwen's reaction to such a blatant remark.

He wasn't disappointed. An attractive blush started above the bodice of her delectable red dress and traveled up her neck to turn her cheeks a bright pink.

He liked that. He liked the sense of innocence that surrounded her.

Maybe her shyness this evening was an attempt to impress his friends, which he could certainly respect. And if that was the case, he probably shouldn't tease her…at least not in any way that his friends might notice.

But there were other ways.… Oh, yes, there were other ways.

The waiters cleared away the first-course dishes and replaced them with gently steaming entrees— thinly sliced strips of beef in a burgundy glaze, lightly salted new potatoes, and crisp string beans sautéed in garlic butter and topped with slivers of almond.

"This looks delicious, Ethan," Lucy commented. "Your caterers are very talented."

"Thank you. I hired them myself," he quipped.

Peter nudged his wife with his elbow. "Didn't I tell you he was smarter than he lets on?"

"You guys are a real laugh riot. Don't listen to them," he told Gwen, shifting his chair an inch more in her direction. "I can actually cook, just nothing like this. And I was *trying—*" he shot his friends a withering glare "—to impress you."

Gwen finished chewing the bite of potato in her mouth and swallowed. "Oh, I'm very impressed. It must have taken nimble fingers and exceptional telephone skills to call up the caterer and hire them for tonight."

"Ho-ho!" Peter let out a gut-level bark of laughter. "Watch out, Ethan. She's got your number already."

"I'm sorry," Gwen said, lowering her gaze and absently laying a palm on his thigh. "That wasn't very nice of me."

Hot flashes of awareness streaked outward from her fingertips, heading straight for his groin. But damned if he was going to let an opportunity like this pass him by.

Quickly, before she could draw her hand back, he covered it with his own and held it in place.

"No, it wasn't," he said softly. "But since my friends' questionable sense of humor seems to be rubbing off on you and I'm the one who made the mistake of inviting them, I won't hold it against you. Besides, you're right. I didn't do much more than pick up the phone and hire these guys to cater a dinner party. You'll just have to let me prove my culinary skills to you some other time."

He looked away from her a moment to scowl at Peter and Lucy. "At my place. *Alone*. Without risk of comment from the peanut gallery."

She flexed her fingers, attempting to pull away, but he held her hand firmly in place. As though nothing out of the ordinary was going on, he picked up his fork with his left hand and continued to eat.

Seconds ticked by before Gwen seemed to realize she wasn't likely to get her hand back without an attention-drawing battle, and she didn't seem willing to cause a scene in front of his friends—which was exactly what he'd been counting on. With a sigh, she relaxed her arm and picked up her own fork.

Ethan concentrated on chewing to cover the grin that threatened. So far, so good.

The atmosphere in the room had shifted subtly, and the four of them ate in silence for several long minutes before Lucy started chatting about the weather and local events in the Georgetown area. God bless Lucy, he thought. She saved the dinner party from dying a painful death, and everyone else from having to rack their brains to come up with small talk.

Ethan nodded and occasionally offered the appropriate response, but the rest of his efforts were concentrated on letting Gwen know just what he had in mind for later. Long after the plates and glasses and flowers and candles had been cleared away. Long after they'd said their good-byes, and Peter and Lucy were on their way home.

Under the table his right hand caressed Gwen's soft, supple skin. The top of her hand, her long, thin fingers, the delicate bones of her wrist. When she didn't rush to pull her palm from his thigh, he moved higher, running the pads of his fingers in a slowly climbing circular motion up the length of her arm.

After reaching her elbow, he surreptitiously slipped his hand onto her thigh, high up where the skirt of her dress bunched from her seated position.

Gwen coughed, then carefully lifted her left hand from his leg and drew her arm back to her side. Surprisingly, she didn't try to dislodge his hand from where it now rested on her thigh.

They were sitting no more than an inch apart, close enough to brush against each other when they moved. Close enough for their knees to touch, which he made a point of doing. Luckily, their proximity and the height of the table kept Peter and Lucy from noticing that he was playing—or trying to play, anyway—with his date, who was directly across from them.

He continued to carry on a fairly intelligent conversation, while at the same time keeping his knee pressed tightly to Gwen's and trailing his hand along the line of her thigh until he reached the scalloped hem of her dress. His fingers fiddled there for a minute, feeling the difference in textures between the lacy overlay of her dress and the silky smoothness of her hosiery.

The catering staff returned then to clear away the dinner plates. Before they came around to his side of the table, Ethan reluctantly removed his hand from Gwen's lap. After all, it wouldn't do for complete strangers to see where his hand was. He shifted in his chair, putting a more respectable distance between them, at least for the moment.

The waiters placed smaller plates in front of each person at the table and then quietly disappeared again.

Ethan had wanted to order tiramisu, a personal favorite and a specialty of the catering company, but he knew it contained alcohol and was afraid Lucy wouldn't be able to eat it in her current condition. So he'd opted for baked Alaska instead.

On the other side of the table, Lucy dug into her ice cream dessert as though she hadn't just devoured a full three-course meal, in addition to an entire vat of beets. He grinned at the look of pure pleasure that crossed her face as soon as the baked Alaska touched her tongue.

"Mmm. This is marvelous." She turned to her husband. "We have to use these people the next time we're in the market for a caterer."

Peter nodded in agreement.

Ethan was about to take a first bite of his own dessert when he felt something brush his leg.

The sensation came again. A flutter of movement that unmistakably became a caress.

Heat lightning struck him, running from his toes all the way up his body. He was surprised the top of his head didn't blow off from the impact. Razor-sharp awareness and longing gathered in his groin, threatening the strength of his zipper.

With his lips tightly locked, he coughed and waited for the ice cream portion of his dessert to melt its way down the back of his throat while he stared at Gwen with bugged-out eyes.

From the smug expression on her face as she continued to enjoy her dessert, he didn't think he was wrong.

This woman, who turned pink at the slightest innuendo and had looked as if she wanted to drive her fork into his fingers when he'd dared to slip his hand under the hem of her skirt, knew exactly what she was doing.

She was suddenly, voluntarily, *wantonly*…playing footsie. With him.

Eight

Inside her head, Gwen did a little happy dance at Ethan's reaction to her stocking-clad toes massaging the hard curve of his anklebone. It brought her more than a little pleasure to see him on the defensive end of a game he'd started.

The turnabout made her feel wild and powerful and sexy…like the woman he thought her to be. The woman she wished she could be in real life.

But for tonight, she *could* be that person, couldn't she? It was expected of her.

Pretending nothing out of the ordinary was taking place on their side of the table, she drew her foot away from Ethan for a moment to shift into a better position to carry out exactly what she had in mind.

Recrossing her right leg over the left, she leaned toward Ethan ever so casually, and then slipped her foot under his pant leg, moving it upward.

"Have you decided on a name for the baby yet?" she asked Lucy and Peter, ignoring—but quite enjoying—the soft strangling sound that came from Ethan's direction.

They chatted for a few minutes while Lucy listed a handful of baby names, and then started arguing with Peter over Emily versus Emma and Adam versus Ian.

Gwen had just worked the hem of Ethan's trousers up a few inches and begun flexing her toes into the tender flesh behind his knee when he scraped his fork across his plate several times, devouring the last of his baked Alaska in two ravenous bites.

"That was great," he announced, slapping his hands together and rubbing them vigorously. "Thanks so much for coming tonight, guys. Hope we can do it again real soon."

Peter and Lucy stared at him, dumbfounded. Their utensils were raised halfway to their mouths, with several bites of dessert remaining on both of their plates.

"Excuse me?" Peter asked, clearly confused. "You begged us to have dinner with you, and now you're asking us to leave?"

"Yeah, sorry about that. I don't mean to be rude, but—"

He paused a second as his eyes went wide, apparently trying to flash his friends some sort of signal. *Get. Out.*

Long seconds ticked past while the four people at the table remained dead silent.

Gwen didn't know what to do. Should she step in and apologize for Ethan's boorish behavior? Or keep her mouth shut and let him deal with his friends on his own?

Finally a knowing smile crossed Lucy's face and she placed a hand on her husband's arm. "Come on, Peter, it's time to go."

"What?" His fork clanked against his plate as it fell from his grip.

"Come *on*," Lucy said, pushing her chair back and then pushing somewhat awkwardly to her feet. "I think what Ethan is trying to say, in his less-than-gentlemanly way, is that he and Gwen would like to be alone."

Peter glanced at Ethan and then threw his napkin down on the table in disgust. "Oh, honestly."

He stood, then began to escort his wife to the door.

"Sorry," Ethan called out as the couple's footsteps clicked a staccato rhythm toward the front entrance of the club. "I'll make it up to you, I promise."

Gwen heard Peter grumble something unintelligible just before the door clicked closed behind them.

She took a deep breath and swallowed, trying to find her voice.

"That wasn't very nice," she chastised. "You didn't need to run them off like that. Or at the very least, you could have walked them to the door."

"Yes, I did," he said simply.

And then he reached out, snagged the leg of her chair, and dragged her none too gently to his side.

"And, no, I couldn't." Taking her hand, he placed it palm down atop his raging erection.

"Can you imagine the reaction I would have gotten if I'd stood up and flashed this? It looks like I'm pitching a tent here."

It did, indeed, look as though he was trying to turn his trousers into a makeshift fort.

"Should I not have teased you the way you were teasing me?" she ventured boldly.

"Oh, you should have," he said in a low rumble. "Just maybe not until after dessert."

"You started it."

Why was her breath coming in shallow little pants? she wondered. And why did her voice have that thin, shuddery quality to it?

"And I intend to finish it. Come here."

Before she could blink, he'd hauled her off her own chair and draped her across his lap, facing him. The stiff prod of his member pressed against the side of her thigh as his arms wrapped about her waist and he tugged her close enough for their mouths to meet.

His lips devoured her, his tongue licking, flicking, diving inside to stroke her own. Excitement bubbled in her belly as his hands moved up and down her spine.

She would be the first to admit she was far from experienced in the act of lovemaking, but she couldn't help thinking that even if she'd been with a hundred other men, she never would have felt the things she was feeling now, with this man.

Her fingers threaded through his dark hair, holding his mouth in place. His warm, strong hand slid over the bare expanse of her chest, and along the curve of a breast. The heat from his fingers burned through the material of her dress, searing her like a brand. His thumb rubbed back and forth along the crest of her breast, driving her crazy, and she moaned at the gut-wrenching need that trickled its way between her legs.

Somewhere behind them, she thought she heard a noise, but the sensations washing through her body overrode anything else. The club could have been crowded with people, all watching their erotic display, and she wouldn't have cared.

But Ethan apparently did. With a reluctant groan, he pulled away, smoothing a hand over her hair as he stared at her puffy, well-loved lips.

He lifted a thumb, running the soft pad along the

lower line of her mouth. "We have an audience," he said in low tones.

She glanced over her shoulder to see one of the catering staff standing several feet away, looking decidedly uncomfortable.

It crossed her mind that she should be embarrassed at being caught in such a shameless situation. She should at least move from Ethan's lap.

But her limbs felt like bags of sand, weighted down by ocean waves, and a slow, delectable warmth was flowing through her veins like brandy on a cold winter's night, making her entirely too complacent.

"For what I want to do next," Ethan murmured near her ear, "we should really be alone. Let's get out of here."

In one liquid motion, Ethan pushed back his chair and stood, setting her on her feet. She wobbled on the one red satin three-inch heel that remained on her foot, her legs feeling like noodles beneath her.

Sensing her loss of equilibrium, Ethan hooked an arm about her waist, picked up her earlier discarded shoe and slipped it on her foot. Then he grabbed her tiny beaded clutch from the table and all but lifted her off the ground as he whisked her toward the rear door.

"We're leaving now," he told the waiter as they passed him. "Stay as long as you need to clean up, and make sure you lock the doors on your way out."

Eyes wide, the young man nodded. And then they

were stalking toward the back of the club, out the rear entrance, to Ethan's car, which glinted silver in the single, bright safety light shining over the parking area.

Unlocking the car with the remote control on his key chain, Ethan opened the passenger side door and practically shoved her inside. A second later he climbed behind the wheel and cranked the key in the ignition.

"My place or yours?" he asked.

For a second she considered letting him take her back to her apartment so he could see the way she lived, see all the signs of the person she really was. But what if he didn't like what he saw and it scared him away?

Oh, she knew there could never be anything permanent between them. Tonight, in fact, would probably be their last night together. The last time she ever saw or heard from him. And as painful as it might be, she could live with that.

She suspected, though, that she was in love with him…had been at least a little in love with him from the moment they met.

But she'd also known from the moment they met that nothing could ever come of a relationship based on lies. She knew who she was and who Ethan was. But he didn't know her. She knew what she wanted and what Ethan wanted, and those desires had them heading in opposite directions.

"Yours," she answered, pushing aside the panic that threatened to ruin an otherwise wonderful—and soon to be spectacular—evening.

She would spend one more night with Ethan. One more night in his arms, making love until neither of them could stand.

A shiver stole through her at the very thought.

Chances were, she'd love him forever…pine for him always…and fail to ever meet another man who lived up to Ethan's image in her mind. Without warning, he'd wormed his way into her heart and taken up residence in a tiny corner of her very soul.

So she would take everything he was willing to give, as much as she could get, and tuck it away in the back of her memory to help her through the next twenty or thirty years.

And then she would die alone…but with a smile on her face because she'd once known the touch of a funny, handsome, amazing man by the name of Ethan Banks.

He broke about fifteen traffic laws on the short drive across town to his apartment, wanting nothing more than to get there and get Gwen into bed. Hell, as stiff as he was right now, they'd be lucky to get the front door closed and make it down to the floor.

An image of her with that hot, red dress hiked up to her waist, back pressed to the wall while he drove

into her again and again, entered his mind, and his
entire body shuddered.

She made him crazy.

Crazy enough to run his friends off before they'd
even finished eating their dinners. To make out like
a horny teenager in front of the gaping catering staff.
To risk life and limb just to get her home and naked—
or maybe not so naked—beneath him.

Tires squealed on pavement as he angled his
Lexus into a parking space behind his building,
braked a mere few inches from the brick wall and cut
the engine.

He was out of the car and on the passenger side
within seconds. Yanking open the door, he grabbed
Gwen's hand and tugged her from the seat, dragging
her behind him as he made a mad dash for the front
doors of his apartment building.

Her shoes scuffed on the ground as she scurried
to keep up, and when he glanced back at her, she was
laughing. Head thrown back, chestnut curls bobbing
around her face, she looked happier than he'd ever
seen her…and sexy enough to be one of those Victoria's Secret runway models.

Damn.

He stopped in his tracks, turning toward her and
grabbing her up as she collided with his chest. Her
amusement was infectious. Burying his nose in her
hair, he chuckled right along with her.

"What's so funny?" he asked. Her hair smelled of strawberries and cream, which only made him want to gulp her down faster.

"You. This. Us."

She drew away slightly, until he was staring into her coffee brown eyes, sparkling with excitement under the dull yellow streetlights.

"What about 'you, this, us'?"

"It's exciting and wild," she told him. "I love that you're in such a hurry to get upstairs. Though my feet might not thank you for it in the morning."

Running his fingers through her long, loose hair, he dropped his gaze to her red satin slippers. "I'll make sure your feet aren't sore from running in those heels. I'll rub your insteps and lick your toes."

She giggled again. Pressed so close, the lithe line of her body rubbed intimately against his throbbing length.

"After," he breathed with a groan, pressing back, letting her know exactly how aroused he was. "I'll give you a full foot massage, I promise. But afterward, okay?"

With a tiny smile gracing her lips, she brushed her nose back and forth along his stubbled cheek. "Okay."

A rush of relief washed over him and he quickly turned around to lead her inside the building. He steered her ahead of him across the carpeted lobby, his hands on her trim waist, his feet shuffling along on the outside of hers while he snuggled close and nuzzled the tender spot just behind her ear.

When the elevator doors slid open, to reveal an empty car, he anticipated the private ride up to his apartment, free to kiss and caress Gwen to his heart's content.

And until the second floor, he did.

The bell dinged, alerting them that the doors were about to open. Tearing his mouth from Gwen's, he glanced up at the lighted panel and saw that they were stopping well before his floor.

"Dammit," he gritted out.

Gwen licked her lips, looking dazed and malleable, just the way he liked her. "What?"

Before he could answer, the doors whispered open and an older gentleman in a tweed jacket stepped into the car. He flashed them both a brief smile and then turned to face the front of the car. Gwen shifted in front of Ethan until she was facing the same direction.

This was the trouble with apartment buildings, Ethan thought. Residents learned early on that it was often easier to ride up with someone else before awaiting the elevator's return trip to the lobby.

But even though they were no longer alone, that didn't mean Ethan couldn't continue to have fun without their uninvited guest being any the wiser.

As they floated silently higher, he buried his nose in the silky strands of hair at the back of Gwen's head and inhaled deeply. The fruity fragrance teased his nostrils and made him hungry for something other than food.

He moved his fingertips down over her hips, to the hem of her skirt, then slipped his hands beneath. She wiggled nervously in an attempt to dislodge his hands. Holding fast, he continued to explore, drawing the material of her dress upward as he straightened.

He had to bite down hard on his tongue to keep from moaning aloud when he discovered the lacy tops of her thigh-high stockings with his roaming fingers. Dipping his head, he bit the tip of her ear to show her how turned on she made him, and then he tugged her shapely fanny tighter against his screaming erection so there could be no doubt.

If there wasn't another person riding upstairs with them, he'd have punched the hold button and taken her right there on the elevator floor.

The next time the tiny interior bell sounded, Ethan looked up to see the number for his floor glowing orange.

"Thank God," he murmured just above Gwen's ear.

The doors opened and he hustled her around the gray-haired man into the hallway. Ethan was already halfway to his apartment digging in his pocket for his keys, when the elevator closed behind them.

As they reached his door, Gwen moved in front of it, leaning back against the painted panel.

"That was interesting," she said with a small smirk. "I admire your restraint."

"Me, too," he muttered.

Honestly, he didn't know how he'd managed to keep from flying apart this long. The keys rattled in his hand, and he was having a hell of a time getting the right one into the lock.

"You didn't tell me you were wearing thigh-highs," he murmured distractedly.

"You didn't ask."

"From now on, consider it a given. I want to know what kind of lingerie you're wearing twenty-four hours a day."

She laughed, the movement causing her petite breasts to jiggle right before his eyes. "Even if I'm wearing granny panties?"

His lips twisted and the damn key finally slid into its hole. "Do you even own granny panties?"

"Every woman owns at least one pair of granny panties, if only because they're so roomy and comfortable."

He made a face, not sure he liked the picture she was painting at all. "All right, not the granny panties. But everything else."

Twisting the knob, he shoved the door open, then snagged her waist with his arm and lifted her off the ground to carry her inside. As soon as the door slammed closed behind them, he spun on his heel and pressed her up against the wooden frame, just as he'd fantasized.

He kissed her, rubbing himself up and down her pelvis like an affectionate cat. She tasted of wine and the baked Alaska they'd eaten for dessert.

"Damn. You're better than a seven-course meal."

Her nails dug into his shoulders, making him even hotter. If that was possible. As it was, he expected steam to come pouring out of his ears at any second.

He licked her jawline, tugged at the soft lobe of her ear and placed wet, nibbling kisses down the column of her neck.

She moaned, letting her head fall back and drawing her leg up so that the heel of her shoe scraped the back of his calf and thigh until her knee was high enough to rest along his hipbone.

"Aren't you going to ask what kind of panties I'm wearing now?"

The words came out thin and tenuous, with that breathy quality he loved. His teeth clenched, and he leaned into the cradle of her thighs, where she'd made more room for him to fit.

He wasn't sure he wanted to know about her panties. He was on the brink of orgasm already. Picturing her in a black satin thong…or red lace Frenchcuts...or even white bikinis could send him straight over the edge.

Then again, the suspense was killing him.

"All right," he panted, "I'll bite. What kind of panties are you wearing right now?"

She looped her arms around his neck, toying with the close-cut hair at his nape. Then she moved her lips close to his ear, her breath making gooseflesh break out along his already perspiration-covered skin.

"I'm not."

For a minute her meaning didn't sink in. And then when it did, he wasn't sure he believed her.

Running his hand under her dress, he passed the top of her seamed thigh-highs and the smooth expanse of her upper thigh, only to have his knuckles come in direct contact with the springy curls covering her mound.

The air froze in his lungs and his gut tightened like a steel drum while several choice expletives flitted through his brain.

"Holy hell, woman," he managed after several long, strangled seconds, "what are you trying to do, kill me?"

"Never that," she said, in the voice Eve likely used to seduce Adam.

"Just trying something new," she added. "And making things a little easier for you, I'd imagine."

"You have no idea."

Reaching into the back pocket of his dress slacks, he retrieved his wallet, flipped open the fine Italian leather, and dug out the condom he kept there for emergency situations. And if this wasn't an emergency situation, he didn't know what was.

"Hold this," he told her.

She took the foil packet out of his hand with her teeth, causing his shaft to jerk with eagerness.

Shaking his head, he let the wallet drop to the floor and began shrugging out of his clothes. The jacket came first, followed by his shirt and belt.

"I hope you don't mind, but I don't think I can make it to the bedroom. I'm going to take you right here, like this, up against the door."

His pants and briefs dropped, and he immediately drove his hands under the fabric of her dress, shoving it up around her waist.

"Tell me now if that's not what you want, because in another few seconds, I won't be able to stop."

Holding his gaze, she tore open the condom wrapper and removed the latex protection. She positioned it at his tip, then rolled the thin barrier slowly down his aching erection.

When that was done, she leaned in and kissed him softly on the lips. "I do want," she whispered.

And then she raised her leg, locking it around his waist, bringing him flush with her moist feminine heat.

One thrust and he was inside. She burned him, her

inner muscles clasping, making him want to weep in pleasure.

Pressing her more firmly into the wooden panel at her back, he lifted her other leg until she was tangled around him like a vine. His hands cradled her buttocks, holding her up and pulling her tighter against him at the same time.

He watched her eyes slide closed, her teeth bite down gently on her bottom lip as he filled her. He couldn't resist leaning forward to lick the seam of her mouth with the tip of his tongue.

That small action turned into a full-blown kiss as his hips angled upward, driving him deeper. He was beyond control, beyond rational thought. His body, along with the mind-numbing ecstasy roaring through it, drove him.

Just when he started to worry that he might come without giving Gwen any pleasure at all, her back arched and she spasmed around him. Her climax was like a lit match being laid to a stick of dynamite, setting off explosions in his blood and in his groin.

He thrust again, harder and harder. Once, twice… The third time, he shot off like a rocket, shouting his triumph into her open mouth and going limp from the amazing force of his release.

Nine

"Don't think any less of me for this," Ethan mumbled in her ear, "but I can't feel my legs, and I think we're about to fall to the floor."

Before she could respond, they did just that. Her back slid halfway down the door until he flipped her around, taking the bottom position and bringing her to straddle him as they collapsed in a pile of limbs and discarded clothes.

She chuckled weakly, resting her head on his shoulder, still feeling him inside her.

Rather than merely becoming a bit more uninhibited, she feared she might be turning into a wanton hussy.

Sex standing up against a wall, not wearing panties in hopes of just such an occurrence… She was
shameless.

And loving every minute of it.

She wasn't foolish enough to think this might be
the first of many such experiences. On the contrary
she knew she had to grab at every new sexual opportunity Ethan offered before they disappeared.

Which was why she'd taken the boutique owner's
advice about leaving her panties at home. It had taken
her several hours to work up the courage, and several quick trips to her underwear drawer to slip a pair
off…then on…then off again. But finally she'd decided her dress was long enough that no one would
know whether or not she was wearing panties unless
she wanted them to.

And apparently Ethan had fully appreciated the
effort.

She certainly had.

Something came over her when she was with him,
something that made her want to jump his bones.

His fingers massaged her head and she rubbed
her cheek comfortingly along his bare, sweat-dap-
pled chest.

"In a minute I'm going to pick you up and carry
you to my bedroom," he murmured sleepily. "Any
minute now."

"Maybe we could each crawl there on our own," she offered, not sure she had that much energy, either.

"Mmm. Maybe we could just sleep here for a couple of hours before going anywhere."

"A couple hours, hmm? Do you really think it will take you that long to recover?"

As though to emphasize her point, her internal muscles clenched of their own volition, and she immediately felt him stir to life within her.

A puff of air hissed through his teeth, his body tensing in her arms.

"Suddenly I'm feeling much more alert," he announced. "A few more seconds, and I'll be raring to go."

She shifted above him in a teasing, seductive way. "I can tell."

"Well, don't do that," he warned, his hands grabbing for her bottom to hold her still. "You're just asking for trouble when you move like that."

"Am I?"

She squirmed again and was rewarded by his harsh intake of breath.

"All right, that's it."

With a superhuman burst of strength, he tilted to one side, then climbed to his feet, taking her with him. She gave a little squeak of surprise and clung to his neck to keep from falling on her behind.

Ethan kicked off his shoes and slacks in the entryway, leaving himself completely naked, then strode across the darkened apartment like Tarzan carrying Jane back to his house in the trees.

"I don't know what kind of magic you're practicing," he whispered below her ear, "but I'm completely transfixed. I want to kiss you all night long. I want to make love to you in every position known to man…and then start over again from the beginning."

She tipped her head back to look at him, wondering how she'd gotten so lucky to land *this* man when she'd decided to lose her virginity on her birthday.

"I'm game," she told him, tightening her grip on his hips with her thighs.

His intense hazel-green eyes locked with hers. "Damn. If we survive the night, we might have to write a whole new version of the *Kama Sutra*."

"That sounds like it would take a lot of hands-on research."

One corner of his mouth lifted in a devilish grin. "Oh, yeah."

She found herself grinning with him and then laughing when he tossed her in the middle of his big bed, only to climb in after her, stalking her like a jungle cat.

He crouched over her prone form and gave a throaty growl, sinking his teeth into the tender flesh between neck and shoulder. She yelped in a mix of pain and delight, and returned the favor by sinking her sharp, manicured nails into the meat of his back.

His lips curled up over his teeth, giving him a dangerous, feral look. Heat stabbed through her, pooling between her legs and making her want him again.

Would she ever get past this insatiable need for him? Would there ever come a day when she could think of him without her insides growing taut with longing?

"Now," he announced, "let's get you undressed. Fully dressed was fun, but naked is even better."

Reaching behind her, he found the tiny zipper of her dress and pulled it down without bothering to lift her from the cushiony mattress. When that was done, he stripped the outfit—jacket and all—from her body and tossed it aside.

He took a moment to admire the scarlet push-up bra encasing her breasts, and the fact that she was bare to the tops of her thigh-highs with their dark seams running in a perfect line down the backs of her legs.

"Someday," he said, his voice thick with emotion, "I'm going to ask you to wear this very outfit while I do wicked things to you. Bra, stockings, do-me heels… But for now, I want to be skin to skin."

Sitting back on his haunches, he raised one of her legs and rested it against his broad chest. He kissed the inside of her ankle, then flipped the red stiletto off her foot and tossed it over his shoulder.

To remove her hose, he started at the snug elastic band that rounded her upper thigh and rolled. His hands worked like a sculptor's on a piece of warm clay, stroking and caressing, sending ripples of desire straight to her core.

She curled her toes and wiggled her bottom closer to his straining manhood, but he wouldn't be rushed. He simply continued to unroll her hosiery, slowly, erotically, until the stocking came free of her foot and fell somewhere amid the clutter of her other garments.

He repeated the same feat on the other leg until she was completely nude, then stretched out on top of her.

The rough hair sprinkled across his pectoral muscles tickled her nipples, causing them to bead and pucker. One of his legs, anchored between both of hers, rubbed gently up and down, bringing nerve endings all along her body to scorching, vibrant life.

He cradled her head in his large palm, the other perched on her hip, his thumb drawing lazy, nonsensical patterns on her flesh. His lips were soft and warm as they trailed around her ear, then over her closed eyelids and the bridge of her nose.

"I could kiss you all day," he said, brushing his mouth across hers as he moved toward her other ear. "Lick you, taste you, nibble you like a rich, buttery pastry."

"Mmm." She craned her neck, allowing him better access, which was about all she seemed capable of at the moment. Her bones felt like jelly, her brain pleasantly numb.

The callused hand that had been resting on her hip suddenly moved upward, sliding over her abdomen, dipping for a moment into her navel, before lightly tracing the underside of her breast.

He knew just where to touch. How soft or firm. How to make her squirm.

Could she do the same? she wondered. Could she make him pant and wiggle and beg?

Her lashes fluttered open only to find him gazing down at her, his hazel eyes a starburst of colors, his expression drawn tight with building passion.

A sudden surge of boldness overcame her and she pushed against his shoulders, twisting them both until they'd traded positions. He was now flat on his back on the mattress with her straddling his hips.

"What are you doing?"

Something she'd always wanted to try, she thought, but said only, "You'll see."

Shimmying lower, she raked her nails along the sculpted lines of his stomach and delighted when he sucked in a sharp breath. His heavy-lidded eyes followed her movement, and from the way his already erect shaft jumped, growing impossibly thicker, she knew he suspected what she had planned.

She'd never done this before, but she'd read several magazine articles that covered the subject, and hoped she could do it at least well enough to bring Ethan pleasure.

Her fingertips toyed with the dark, springy curls surrounding his manhood, experimentally touching the twin sacs pulled up tight against his body. And then her hand circled the base of his arousal, holding it still while she lowered her mouth and licked the very tip.

She felt the shudder roll through him and took it as encouragement. Her hair fell about her head, dusting his thighs as she took the rest of his length between her lips.

She reveled at the difference in textures he seemed to encompass. Soft, yet hard, like velvet covering steel.

He filled her mouth and she shivered with excitement, feeling somehow more powerful and womanly than ever, now that she knew she could bring this sort of pleasure to him.

He flexed beneath her, his body stretching and arching like the bow of a violin.

"Gwen."

His hands tangled in her hair, both holding her in place and trying to draw her away. She ignored him, continuing to lick and suck his stiff shaft.

"Gwen, sweetheart." This time he tugged harder, until she faced him.

"If you don't stop," he told her in a gravelly tone, "I'm going to come. And I don't want to do that without you."

She smiled and climbed back up his body, kissing him deeply when he reached for her and drew her mouth down to his.

Sitting back, she wiggled until she felt the tip of him slipping along her opening and let it slide straight into her. She loved the feel of that long, hard length of steel filling her so fully.

His hips arched beneath her, driving him even farther inside, and she rode him. Slow and easy, their lips still locked, her breasts swaying between them.

He let out a low groan, his fingers digging into the flesh of her upper arms, and then suddenly, he froze.

"Wait," he gasped.

Tightening his grasp on her arms, he lifted her bodily away from him. He pushed her back, at the same time moving until he could lean against the headboard.

"I'm sorry," he told her, his chest rising and falling with the effort it took to draw air into his lungs. "I didn't mean to push you away, but we couldn't keep going like that."

Cocking her head to the side, she waited for him to explain, since she'd thought things were going pretty darn well.

"I'm not wearing protection," he said finally.

Gwen looked down at his uncovered manhood, and then back up to meet his eyes.

What had she done? she thought, as the gravity of

the situation began to sink in. A minute or two more, and they both could have been in big trouble.

She was pretending to be this worldly, knowledgeable woman, but it was suddenly clear she knew next to nothing about having casual sex.

All she needed was to wind up pregnant to some guy she'd met in a bar. Even if her heart told her Ethan was much more than just "some guy."

Her heart wouldn't be the one seen as an unwed mother. Her heart wouldn't have to deal with the very real possibility that Ethan would want nothing to do with her after tonight, even if she did wind up pregnant. And her heart certainly wouldn't be the one raising a child alone.

Not that having a child—Ethan's child—wouldn't give her some sort of comfort. She could have a piece of him, then, to keep near her always and remind her of the short span of time when he'd made her feel truly alive.

Gwen gave herself a mental shake. What was wrong with her? She wasn't some adolescent girl who believed a baby was going to solve all her problems or tie a man to her forever. She was an adult, and even if her decisions lately hadn't been the smartest she'd ever made, she certainly didn't need to add another blunder to her list of sins. She would have to be more careful.

"It's all right," Ethan said, drawing her out of her

inner turmoil. "I don't think we went far enough that we need to worry."

Leaning across the disheveled bedding, he reached into the nightstand for a condom packet and waved it triumphantly in the air. "We won't be taking any more chances, though."

When she didn't respond, he smoothed a hand through her hair and scooted forward to kiss her gently on the lips. "Really. I think we're okay."

Swallowing past the lump of emotion lodged in her throat, she nodded. No, they wouldn't take any more chances. And, no, they weren't okay. Because, come morning, she could no longer continue with her lies, which meant that the relationship would end. But she had this last night with Ethan, and she tried valiantly to reclaim the passion and excitement that had been coursing through her veins only moments before.

His lips quirked in a devilish smile as he looked at her, and she knew he had some kind of trick up his sleeve.

"Since you seem to be feeling adventurous tonight," he whispered in a husky tone, "will you let me take you from behind?"

A ripple of excitement washed over her as she imagined him doing just that. It would be another first. Another daring, wanton activity she might never experience again.

Because she couldn't imagine trusting any lover but Ethan.

"All right," she answered before she had time to change her mind.

He pressed his lips to her forehead, then slowly eased out from under her while she wrapped her arms around one of the bed's fluffy pillows and lowered herself onto her belly on the warm, satiny sheets.

Pulling the hair away from her face, he kissed her cheek and nape before letting his lips trail the long line of her spine. At the same time, she heard him tear open the condom wrapper and cover himself with the thin layer of protection.

A moment later, his hands were on her bare flesh, teasing her breasts and waist and the heat between her legs.

"You can tell me to stop at any time," he whispered.

The words vibrated along her skin where his lips caressed her.

She didn't think stopping was an option. Already, she could feel her feminine channel moistening and tightening in anticipation.

Gently, he lifted her hips. Her head and shoulders remained on the bed, comfortably cushioned by the navy satin bedclothes.

He leaned forward, kissing her shoulder while one hand cupped her breast, the other dipping into her wet warmth. His fingers found the tight little bud hidden within her curls and stroked it expertly, making her moan and arch her hips even higher. Knowing she was more than ready for anything he might do, he found her opening and slipped inside.

Gwen gasped as he filled her, loving the sensations he created in this reverse position. He held himself still for a moment, though she could feel the restraint it took in the tautness of his muscles everywhere they touched.

"Are you all right?" he asked.

She rolled her head on the sheets, letting him know she was. Possibly more than all right. Warm molasses was pouring through her veins, even as sharp bursts of sensation sparked, making her feel alive and aware.

Once he knew she was okay, he started moving slowly in and out, coordinating the motion of his hips with the dance of his fingers within her folds. Fire built low in her belly with each hard thrust of his steely length deep inside, and the rub of his callused fingertips on the swollen button of her desire.

She found herself rising up on the heels of her hands, wanting to be more involved, wanting to be closer. When Ethan drove forward, she drove back until they were moving in tandem, gasping for air, reaching for completion.

Her stomach tightened, her internal muscles following suit. And then she was flying over the edge, immeasurable pleasure coursing through her as she cried out his name.

Behind her, she felt Ethan stiffen. His fingers locked onto her hips like talons as he climaxed inside her with a guttural moan.

Seconds later they fell onto the bed in a tangle of limp, sweaty limbs.

Ethan fumbled beneath their exhausted forms until he'd loosened the sheets and covered them both. His arms wrapped around her, and she rested her head on his shoulder, her breath still ragged from exertion and the intensity of the orgasm he'd just wrung from her.

His fingers combed distractedly through the hair at her temples, lulling her even deeper toward sleep, and she wished things could always be like this between them.

She wished he knew the real Gwen Thomas, and was as attracted to her as he seemed to be to the Gwen he thought she was. Or she wished her alter ego's personality was her own so that there was nothing to hide from him.

But she'd already started down the wrong road with him and didn't see any way to go back. If she could, though, she would do whatever it took to stay in this relationship, to build something real and lasting with him.

Provided he was interested, of course. Because

now she knew for sure...she didn't just lust after him, didn't just think she *might* be in love.

Somewhere between the first night she'd walked into The Hot Spot and now, she'd fallen head over heels, no-other-man-will-ever-do in love with him. She wanted to stay with him—in his bed, in his arms, in his life—forever.

It wasn't to be, of course. She knew that. But a girl could dream.

A few hours later Gwen blinked awake in the inky darkness. Ethan was stretched out beside her. His chest rose and fell steadily with his even breathing, and for long minutes she simply watched him while he slept.

Glancing at the digital clock on the bedside table, she saw that it was nearly 3:00 a.m.

She felt like Cinderella, running late at the ball. If she stayed until morning, she was likely to turn back into a charwoman. But if she left now, Ethan would continue to believe she'd been a beautiful— if temporary—princess.

Her heart squeezed at the thought of never seeing him again, but she didn't have a choice. It was better to go now, with the memories of their time together pleasant and fresh in her mind.

Before he found out who she really was, and began to hate her for lying to him.

Lifting the sheet, she gently extricated herself from Ethan's hold, peeling her arm from his chest, sliding her leg out from under his. When she lowered her bare feet over the edge of the bed, they sank into the plush carpeting.

Sneaking around in the dark, she collected her clothing by the trickle of moonlight shining through a single window on the far side of the room. She looked to the bed as she fastened her bra and shimmied into her dress, reassuring herself that Ethan was still asleep. She stuck her feet into the high heels, not bothering with stockings. Those she stuffed into her tiny clutch, which she'd found on his black lacquer dresser.

She was halfway into the hall but couldn't bring herself to leave. Not just yet.

Tiptoeing back to the bed, she leaned over Ethan's still form.

"Goodbye," she whispered, tears springing to her eyes.

She kissed the tips of her fingers and pressed them lightly to his stubbled cheek. "I love you."

He never moved, never gave any sign that she'd woken him or that he'd heard her heartfelt declaration. And that was for the best, she knew.

Before she broke into uncontrolled sobs, she hurried from the room and out of the apartment…just like Cinderella running from her handsome Prince Charming.

Ten

Ethan rolled over in bed, his arm stretching out for the woman he knew should be there beside him. Unlike the last time he'd expected to wake up with Gwen, this time he knew, deep down in his gut, that she wasn't there.

Dammit. What was it with this woman that she couldn't stay in bed through the night? He swore the next time he managed to get her into bed, he wasn't ever letting go of her again.

Pushing himself up on his elbows, he sat stunned for a moment.

Had he just admitted, even silently, that he didn't want to be rid of Gwen? That, in fact, he wished she were still here, close to him, ready to share the day?

Her scent still surrounded him. It was on his skin and on his sheets. In his nostrils and pores and soul.

But it was more than the physical. It was the way she made him feel, and how he woke up in the mornings wondering when he would next see her. *Wanting* to see her.

That didn't mean he wanted to *be* with her, though. Did it?

"All right, Banks," he told himself, striving for calm. "Think about this. Think long and hard."

Did wanting to see Gwen every chance he got—basically wanting to be with her twenty-four hours a day—mean he was ready to make things exclusive? Maybe even…permanent?

He waited for the customary panic to overtake him. Waited for his brain to conjure the memory of Susan's betrayal and to think about all the women he'd be foregoing at the club if he committed to an exclusive relationship.

Nothing. No panic, no cause for regret.

He thought about Susan and how it had felt when she'd left him. Usually, white-hot anger and resentment followed, pretty much putting him in a lousy mood for the rest of the day.

Now, however, he found himself feeling…nothing. Yeah, Susan was a part of his past, his marriage to her something he definitely wouldn't do again if he had the chance. But the thought of her, and how she'd used him, didn't seem to send his blood pressure soaring anymore.

Interesting.

Then he thought of Gwen, and a warm, soothing sensation flowed over him. He realized—quite suddenly and with utmost certainty—that Gwen was *not* Susan, in any way, shape, or form.

He pictured Gwen's long brown hair and the touch of a smile that always seemed to grace her lips. He heard her laugh, and experienced the same rush of adrenaline that always washed over him when she was with him.

From there, his mind turned to a possible future, if he and Gwen stayed together.

He saw her hand linked with his, their bodies brushing as they walked together. He saw her curled up on the couch in his office at the club while he worked at his desk, or at the end of the bar, sipping a fruity pink drink while he took orders behind the bar.

He saw her in his apartment, making herself at home. He saw her walking down the aisle of a church where he waited to make her his bride. And then he saw them several years down the road, two or three children dancing around a Christmas tree while he and Gwen stood back, watching them open the presents Santa had brought, even though they'd spent all of December tracking them down.

Oh, my God. He was in love with her.

Once again he waited for the panic to come, but once again it didn't. An immediate sense of contentment settled into every fragment of his being instead.

For the first time since Susan had left him, he wasn't afraid of getting serious with a woman.

He wasn't afraid of the idea of marriage and family.

And he most especially wasn't afraid of *love*.

Cursing, he sat up on the edge of the bed, driving his fingers through his hair in frustration. Great. He finally figured out that he was in love with Gwen Thomas and she'd run out on him—again.

Well, he had no intention of letting her go.

Tossing back the covers, he stalked to the master bathroom and jumped in the shower, taking the fastest scrub in history.

He'd had a list of errands three pages long to run today, but those tasks had suddenly narrowed to one all-important goal: *find Gwen.*

He toweled off, then stood in front of the medicine-cabinet mirror, shaving as quickly as he could without causing major blood loss. As it was, he ended up with a dozen nicks.

After applying aftershave and deodorant, he marched to the dresser for a T-shirt and jeans. Once he'd donned his socks and shoes, he scooped up his car keys and cell phone and was out the door.

He headed straight for Gwen's apartment, using his hands-free cell phone to make a couple of calls on the way. One to his day manager at the club, asking her to take care of the paperwork and errands Ethan had planned to cover, then another to his night manager to let him know he could be reached on his cell.

By that time he was in Gwen's neighborhood. He pulled into the first available space he could find near her building and took off down the sidewalk at a near jog.

He rang the bell for Gwen's apartment. There was no response, but he wasn't taking no for an answer.

He laid on the button again, but when another resident came out of the building, he waited for her to pass out of sight, then deftly caught the door before it could close. Slipping inside, he took the stairs two at a time up to Gwen's apartment and started knocking. A few minutes later he realized she was either avoiding him or she really wasn't home.

"Come on, Gwen," he called through the wooden panel, hoping against hope. "Open up."

Down the hall, hinges creaked, and he turned his head to see a little old lady with tight white curls peering out of her opened door.

"I'm sorry, young man, but Gwen isn't home."

Abandoning his post at Gwen's apartment, he took a few steps in the older woman's direction. When he saw her shrink back, he slowed his gait, not wanting to alarm her.

"Do you know where I can find her?" he asked. "It's important."

She eyed him up and down warily, never poking more than her head out into the hallway. "Well, I suppose she's at work, same as every other day."

Work. Damn. She was probably driving all over creation, looking for new and unique clothing designs for her job as a buyer.

"Do you have any idea where she might be, exactly? Or how I can reach her?"

"Sure, she just works down the street at the library. Do you know where it is?"

Ethan blinked, trying to process the woman's words. "The library?" he questioned aloud.

Gwen had said she was a fashion buyer for several of the more upscale stores in the city and some of the boutiques in town. What would she be doing at the local library?

"That's right. She should be there, unless she's out to lunch already."

He glanced at his watch. Ten o'clock in the morning was awfully early for lunch. Good, then maybe he could catch her.

"Thank you." He lifted a hand, waving in appreciation before he turned and hurried down the stairs.

Rather than move his car and risk not being able to find another parking spot, he walked the several blocks to the Georgetown branch of the D.C. Library.

Come to think of it, Gwen had been descending the steps of the public library that first day he'd spotted her and followed her back to her apartment building.

He didn't know what was going on, exactly, but he honestly didn't care. The important thing was finding Gwen and telling her how he felt about her.

Not to mention figuring out how she felt about him.

It took him under five minutes to reach the colonial redbrick building. A white cupola loomed above him, with towering pillars marking the entrance. He took the wide front steps in two strides and yanked open the door, holding it for a moment so that another patron could exit.

The silence inside was deafening. He was used to the pounding, ear-splitting environment at The Hot Spot. Even when he was working alone in his office or driving in the car, he usually had some kind of music on in the background.

But this was the type of quiet he only experienced in the first thirty seconds after arriving home, or entering the club before opening—the lull before flipping on the television or sound system.

He stood inside the main entrance, staring at rows upon rows of high shelving, cluttered with books. At tables with four or six chairs around each, an assortment of people were reading.

Along the far wall, individual carrels held large,

funny-looking machines that he thought he remembered being used for microfiche.

And then there was the waist-high circulation desk, with a librarian behind it. A librarian who wasn't Gwen.

This middle-aged woman had her dark hair up in a bun and wore a light blue sweater over a flowered blouse. She was trying to look busy, while at the same time watching him through large-framed glasses.

He hadn't seen Gwen during his quick perusal of the library, so he stepped up to the counter and smiled when the librarian pretended to finally notice him.

"Can I help you?" She smiled politely, her voice barely above a whisper.

"Yes, I need to speak to someone, and I was told she might be here. Her name is Gwen Thomas. She has beautiful chestnut hair that hangs to her shoulders in waves. In a word, she's hot. Does she work here, by chance?"

The woman's eyes, he noticed, had gone wide behind her plastic-rimmed glasses.

"Um…we do have a Gwen Thomas who works here," she said, sounding decidedly uncomfortable. "But I'm not sure she's the same person you're looking for. Our Gwen is a pretty girl, though."

His heart sank. He didn't know how many Gwen Thomases there were in the world, let alone the

Georgetown area, but he felt certain that if his Gwen worked here, the woman behind the desk would know it.

There was no way *his* Gwen could ever be mistaken for anyone else, and she definitely couldn't be confused with simply "a pretty girl." *His* Gwen was a knockout.

"Oh, here she is now," the woman announced suddenly.

He swung around, coming face-to-face with Gwen. *His* Gwen.

She wasn't dressed as he'd come to expect from her, but she still looked good. Damn good, and as sexy as always in a formfitting, daffodil-yellow knit dress with short sleeves, a scoop neckline and a hem that hit her about five inches above the knee. A large, painted daisy pin decorated the space between shoulder and left breast, and in her right arm she carried a stack of thick, well-worn hardcover books.

"Ethan." Her face went three shades paler when she saw him, her voice cracking over his name. "What are you doing here?"

A thousand questions of his own raced through his head, starting with *What are* you *doing here?* and *I thought you were a fashion buyer, not a librarian.* But none of those were nearly as important as his real reason for tracking her down.

"Looking for you."

He tapped his palm on the oaken countertop and offered the older librarian a hasty "Thank you" before moving to stand directly before Gwen.

"Why did you leave this morning?" he asked pointedly, but low enough that no one else could hear, even in the dead silence surrounding them.

She blushed slightly and juggled the books she was holding, which must have been growing heavy. He took them, three at a time, and set them on the nearest tabletop until her arms were empty.

"Is there someplace more private where we can talk?"

He didn't know about her, but he wasn't eager to have his personal life play out in front of everyone in the Georgetown Public Library.

There were more people here than he'd have expected on a weekday morning. Of course, he hadn't been in a library since high school, so he wasn't exactly an authority on the subject.

She glanced around and then nodded, turning to lead him to a small, glass-paneled room hidden behind the stacks. Once they were inside, she closed the door with a quiet click and drew the blinds to hide them from curious onlookers.

He leaned back against the edge of a cluttered metal desk and crossed his arms over his chest. She didn't look any more comfortable about his sudden appearance when she faced him again.

"Are you going to answer my question?" he asked calmly.

"What question?" She ran her hands down the front of her dress nervously, refusing to meet his gaze.

"Why did you leave this morning?" he repeated.

"Was I supposed to stay?"

"If you had to go to work or something, you could have woken me to let me know or left a note saying what time you'd be back. Otherwise, I sort of expected to wake up and find the woman I'd gone to sleep with the night before still in my bed."

It hit him, not for the first time, that he never usually expected to wake up beside the woman he'd gone to bed with the night before. But then, being in love with Gwen changed everything, didn't it?

"I'm sorry," she said. "I wouldn't have known what to say."

He eyed her warily, getting a funny feeling in the pit of his stomach. "You never intended to come back, did you? Or call me, or see me again."

Taking her silence and the nervous licking of her lips as answer enough, he balled his hands into fists to keep from rubbing the painful spot directly over his heart.

"That's great. Just great," he ranted. "I've spent these last weeks thinking about you constantly, dreaming about you, coming to terms with the fact that I'm finally over my ex-wife's betrayal and falling seriously in love with you, while you were using me for nothing more than a momentary amusement."

Gwen's heart froze in her chest, then picked up its beat with a vengeance, pounding against her rib cage as though it was trying to break free.

It had been startling enough to walk out of the stacks and find him standing in front of the circulation desk, looking drop-dead gorgeous—as usual—in a pair of worn jeans and a rusty orange T-shirt that molded to his chest and biceps like a second skin. But now he was standing in front of her, complaining that she hadn't been there when he awakened this morning and…*telling her he might seriously be falling in love with her?*

Was she hearing him correctly? Had he just said what she thought he'd said?

No. She had to be mistaken. He couldn't have just said he was falling in love with her. Men like him didn't fall in love with women like her.

But her brain was telling her those were the words he'd uttered, and she had to know for sure.

"What did you say?" she asked breathlessly, her diaphragm tightening with fear that he might deny it.

He rolled his eyes in annoyance. "You used me for your own amusement—"

She shook her head violently, taking a tentative step toward him. Her lungs didn't seem capable of drawing air.

"Before that. Did you say… Did you say you were falling in love with me?"

"Yeah," he admitted reluctantly, his eyes narrowing. "But I'm sure as hell not going to say it again. I've had enough humiliation for one day, thanks very much."

Ignoring his rant, she moved closer, fighting the urge to reach out and touch him.

"Do you still feel that way?" she asked in a voice smaller than she'd ever heard herself speak before.

"What do you care? You sneaked out this morning so you wouldn't have to face me in the bright light of day."

She swallowed hard. "You're right. That's exactly why I left. But only because I didn't think you'd ever want to see me again. I know the kind of guy you are, Ethan. You own a nightclub. You meet hundreds of gorgeous women every night. I'm sure any number of them jump at the chance to go home with you."

"What's your point? I met you at my club, and you came home with me the same night."

"I know that. I didn't mean to sound critical."

If anything, his sex appeal was exactly what had drawn her to him. She'd wanted a man to make love to her without asking a lot of questions or expecting more from the encounter. But somehow she'd still gotten too deeply involved, too emotionally attached to the man she'd chosen. Or, more accurately, the man who'd chosen her.

"To be honest," she continued, "I didn't think you'd want a woman like me hanging around too long. I thought you'd be just as happy to be rid of me."

He watched her intently for several long seconds, and then he kicked away from the desk, where he'd been perched ever since they entered the room.

"What do you mean, 'a woman like you'?"

"A woman like me. A plain, boring librarian who had never set foot inside a nightclub before my birthday."

"I thought you were a fashion buyer."

"I lied. I didn't think you or your friends would be very impressed if you knew I spent my days shelving books and helping students with their research."

"Why the hell would I care what you did for a living?" he demanded. "I'll admit I'm surprised, but more that you felt the need to lie about your job than by the job itself. And where the hell do you get off saying you're 'plain' and 'boring'? We haven't been seeing each other long, but I've never known you to be either of those things."

"That's just it, Ethan. You don't know me, not at all. Everything about me—everything *you* know about me—has been made up. That night I walked into your club for the first time, I'd had my hair colored and bought a new outfit completely different from my usual style because I was depressed about turning thirty-one and wanted to do something wild and outrageous for once in my life. *You* were my chance to be uninhibited and spend the evening with a fun, handsome man who wouldn't think twice about me the next day."

She gave a little laugh that came out more like a huff and ran her fingers through her hair in agitation.

"But you weren't at all what I expected. You were sweet and kind and didn't just use me for sex. You actually tracked me down at home and asked me out again. You acted like you wanted to get to know me better, when I expected to be nothing more to you than a one-night stand."

Ethan shook his head, looking bewildered. "You're telling me you ran off this morning because I was paying *too* much attention to you? Because I wasn't a first-class heel and treated you like a woman I was in a relationship with rather than someone I'd used for a quick lay?"

"No. No, you don't understand. There's nothing wrong with you. You were wonderful, just not at all what I'd expected or planned for."

She sighed in frustration. "What I'm saying is that the woman you met that night at your club isn't me. And when you showed up at my apartment and invited me to dinner, I had to keep pretending that I was worldly and confident. I had to buy more sexy, revealing outfits, and make up another occupation so you wouldn't know I spend my days here, surrounded by books."

Ethan thought he'd been confused this morning when he suddenly realized he was in love with Gwen. Now, though, he was truly perplexed. She seemed to think that the woman he'd been spending so much time with and the woman she was on her own were two different people.

But he knew different. He knew that even if she'd been pretending to be someone else at the club the first night they'd met, there was still some part of that sexy, vibrant woman inside of her now. He knew that just because she was a librarian by profession didn't mean she was boring or dull. And he knew that what she did and how she saw herself had nothing to do with the woman he'd fallen in love with.

Frankly, he was relieved to discover she'd run out on him only because she didn't think she could live up to his expectations or his lifestyle. For a while there, he'd been afraid she didn't really care for him.

He supposed he should be angry that she'd lied to him at all, but he couldn't seem to bring himself to care about that right now. Not considering the bigger issue.

Reaching out, he stroked his hands down her bare arms, feeling the nervous shudder that rippled through her petite frame.

"I only have one question," he told her, keeping his tone low but solemn. "Did you lie about this?"

Without warning, he pulled her against him and covered her mouth with his own. His tongue thrust between her lips, circling and stroking, tangling with hers.

It felt like forever since he'd last kissed her, desire flaring hot and fast between them. He wrapped his arms around her waist to draw her even closer, encouraged when the tension seemed to drain from her lithe form and she went limp in his embrace.

It wasn't easy, but he forced himself to pull away, breaking the kiss and taking a step back so he wouldn't be tempted to grab her up again.

"Was that pretend?" he asked. "Was the time you spent in my arms and in my bed an act?"

She looked stunned, her eyes somewhat glazed. But her head was already moving in vehement denial. "No. I promise that was real, every bit of it."

His heart suddenly felt fifty pounds lighter, floating in his chest like a helium balloon. He wanted to throw his head back and shout with joy. Lift his hands and dance like Rocky at the top of those wide Philadelphia steps.

Instead, he grinned and lifted one of her hands to his mouth, pressing his lips to the smooth ridge of her knuckles.

"Then I don't care about anything else. I love *you*, not your job or your clothes. You could work at a burger joint and wear a little paper hat, for all I care."

That brought a smile to her face, though she still looked uncertain.

"I'm not who you thought I was, though," she insisted, her eyes growing misty. "I collect ceramic kitty cat figurines and spend most of my evenings reading, not club hopping."

"Do you love me, Gwen?" he asked point-blank. "That's all I want to know. Do you love me?"

Her lower lip quivered, but she answered immediately and without hesitation. "Yes, I love you. I didn't want to, I tried to fight it, but, God help me, I do."

One arm snaked around her and he pulled her flush with his body, kissing her again until they were both breathless. When they finally broke apart, it was only to suck in lungfuls of much-needed oxygen. Now that he had her where he wanted her, he wasn't ever letting her go.

"But, Ethan—"

"No." He held up a hand, cutting her off. "No more excuses, no more reasons why I can't possibly have feelings for you. It took me a hell of a long time to get past my bitterness with Susan and realize I could actually open myself to loving another woman. I want you, ceramic cats, library card and all. I'll even cut back on my hours at the club, if it will make you more comfortable. I've been looking into opening a second location, anyway, so I can just as easily spend my time on that."

"You don't have to change anything for me," she whispered. "Except for maybe sleeping with strange women the first night you meet them."

She gazed up at him adoringly, a teasing tilt to her lips, and he knew he was watching her with much the same expression in his eyes.

"Deal. And the same thing goes for you. From now on, I'm a one-woman man and you're a one-man woman."

The happiness in her face grew until she was positively glowing. She leaned up on tiptoe to press her lips to his.

"Deal."

Epilogue

Gwen shifted on the sofa in Ethan's office, turning the page of her favorite battered paperback copy of *Jane Eyre*. She could feel the pounding rhythm from the main club area vibrating through the floor, but this room was practically soundproof, and she had long ago learned to ignore the strange sensation of knowing what song was playing without really hearing it.

She'd learned a lot of things over the past several months. Such as what it was like to live with a man, and that Ethan truly did love her—just the way she was.

They'd moved in together soon after Ethan's sudden appearance at the library and their mutual admissions of love. But she'd still been nervous and had doubts, considering the misconceptions they'd been functioning under ever since they met. So they'd agreed to take things slowly and really get to know each other before jumping into anything permanent.

Ironically, Ethan had moved into *her* apartment—bookshelves, cat figurines, and all—instead of the other way around. He claimed to like the homier, more sedate decor, and to be tired of his bachelor pad, which he'd sublet until his lease expired.

After six months of being together practically every minute they weren't at work, Gwen felt confident that Ethan really did know her, inside and out. And she knew him. Which was why, when Ethan took her out for a candlelit dinner and asked her to marry him, she'd had no reservations about saying yes. *Yes, yes, a thousand times yes.*

They'd been married at Jazz Hot, Ethan's newest business venture. He'd found an old warehouse on the other side of town and had it completely renovated to resemble the old jazz clubs of the forties and fifties, all in black-and-white art deco.

Before the grand opening, they'd exchanged vows on the empty stage, decorated with balloons and streamers in the club's trademark colors. Afterward, their friends and families joined them for a buffet dinner, followed by dancing long into the night.

That had been almost a year ago, and she couldn't

remember ever being happier. She had a new husband, a new home, and big news to tell Ethan.

From the corner of her eye, Gwen caught the light from her reading lamp reflecting off the diamond-and-gold bands on her left ring finger. She smiled, twisting the bands slightly, as she thought about surprising Ethan.

Just then the office door opened and Ethan strode inside, bringing the downstairs noise with him until the door was firmly closed again.

"Hey," he said softly, smiling that warm, loving smile that always caused her heart to flip over in her chest. "Don't let me interrupt your reading."

Marking her page, she set the book aside and sat up. "That's all right. I couldn't concentrate, anyway."

He crossed the room and pulled her to her feet for a quick kiss. "Music bothering you?"

"Nope," she said, wrapping her arms around his neck and kissing him back. "I was thinking."

"About what?"

"You, and how much I love you."

"Is that right?" He glanced over her shoulder to where the book lay. "Should I apologize for tearing you away from Jane and Mr. Rochester?"

She grinned, warmth spreading outward from the center of her chest. "You've been reading behind my back."

"I've got to keep up with my little librarian wife,

don't I? And for your information, I liked the story. I'm halfway through *Wuthering Heights* now."

If possible—and she didn't think it was—she loved him even more for taking an interest in her job, as well as one of her greatest passions.

"I'm impressed."

"Mmm." He nuzzled the side of her neck. "Enough to tuck me into bed tonight and tell me a story?"

"You want me to read to you?" she asked with some surprise. That was something they hadn't tried yet. Not that it wouldn't be fun.

"Not necessarily. I was thinking you could make something up. Something sexy and naughty."

"Ah, you want me to play Scheherazade."

"*Arabian Nights,* right?" he asked, looking eager for her answer.

She grinned. "Right. You're not ready to go home yet, though, are you?"

The clock on the wall showed it was much earlier than he usually left the club on busy nights like tonight.

"I do have a few things to take care of yet, but I shouldn't be much longer. You're not too tired to hang around, are you? I can call you a cab, if you are. Or run you home, then come back."

"No, I'm fine," she told him, shaking her head and watching as he moved to take a seat behind his wide desk.

Surprisingly, she felt great, for being in her first trimester. Perhaps that was why Ethan hadn't noticed her condition yet. She was anxious to see his reaction when he found out he was going to be a daddy.

"Ethan," she said, rounding his desk and resting a hip on its edge.

She was nervous, despite the fact that she knew he wasn't opposed to having children. That was only one of the many things they'd discussed during their lengthy get-to-know-you period. She just didn't know how he would feel about her getting pregnant so soon.

Leaning back in his chair, he covered her denim-clad knee with a large palm and began stroking small circles with his thumb. His gaze held hers as he waited for her to continue.

"I have a surprise for you, and I'm hoping you'll be happy about it."

The corners of his mouth curved up in amusement. "You didn't use the credit card to charge more furniture for the new house, did you? If you keep shopping, I don't know where we'll put it all."

"No, nothing like that."

Although, they would have to do a bit more shopping in the ensuing months if they hoped to have the nursery ready before the baby was born. But then, they'd been doing a lot of decorating since moving into their new two-story, refurbished Tudor-style house.

A note of seriousness slipped into his voice as he sensed that whatever she had to tell him had her feeling anxious. "Okay, what is it?"

She took a deep breath and dove in, much as she had the night of her thirty-first birthday.

But look how well that had turned out.

With a smile, she mouthed the words, "I'm pregnant."

He blinked, otherwise remaining perfectly still for several long seconds. "Excuse me?"

"Pregnant. I'm pregnant. We're going to have a baby."

"I thought that's what you said," he mumbled, a dazed expression falling over his face. "Are you sure?"

"Very sure," she told him, still waiting for his full reaction. "I took a home pregnancy test and saw the doctor. Both were positive. I'm six weeks along, and if you don't tell me pretty soon whether you're happy or upset, I just might burst into tears."

A beat passed, and then he grabbed her up, kissing her with a love and passion she'd never known before meeting him. His fingers flexed on her belly, warming her straight through her top and jeans.

"I'm happy," he murmured against her mouth once he'd released her. "Happier than I've ever been in my life. A little scared about being a father, but still…happy."

She gazed into his eyes and smiled. "You'll be a

great father," she assured him. "And we have almost eight months to learn everything we need to know and get over being scared. Lucy and Peter can help us out, too, I'm sure."

Ethan rolled his eyes. "In that case, I'm in trouble. I gave Peter a rough time when he was nervous about impending fatherhood. I can only imagine how much fun he'll have repaying the favor."

"Maybe if you offer to babysit little Shane a couple times, he'll forgive you. He and Lucy have been trying to get some alone time for a while now."

"Babysitting, huh? Will you come with me and help me out?"

"Of course. It will be good practice."

Minutes ticked by while he stared intently at the area of her belly, rubbing his hand tenderly over the spot where their child nestled.

"A baby," he breathed with wonder. "I can't believe it." And then he raised his gaze to hers. "You've made all my dreams come true, Gwen. I hope you know that."

Tears welled in her eyes, but no matter how hard she tried, she couldn't hold them back.

"Oh, no," she said, waving a hand in front of her face. "I think this is one of those pregnant crying jags I was warned about."

She threw her arms around his neck and hugged him tight. "You've made all my dreams come true, too. Dreams I didn't even know I had. I love you, Ethan."

"I love you, too, sweetheart," he whispered just before his mouth molded to hers.

When they finally got home that night and climbed into bed, Ethan was the one who told her a story…the story of a shy princess and a lonely prince who found each other, fell in love and lived happily ever after.

* * * * *

Look for Heidi Betts's next Silhouette Desire available February 2006!

Silhouette Desire

A violent storm.

A warm cabin.

One bed...for two strangers
stranded overnight.

Author

Bronwyn Jameson's

latest PRINCES OF THE OUTBACK novel
will sweep you off your feet and into
a world of privilege and passion!

Don't miss

The Ruthless Groom

Silhouette Desire #1691
Available November 2005

Only from Silhouette Books!

If you enjoyed what you just read,
then we've got an offer you can't resist!

Take 2 bestselling love stories FREE!

Plus get a FREE surprise gift!

Clip this page and mail it to Silhouette Reader Service™

IN U.S.A.	IN CANADA
3010 Walden Ave.	P.O. Box 609
P.O. Box 1867	Fort Erie, Ontario
Buffalo, N.Y. 14240-1867	L2A 5X3

YES! Please send me 2 free Silhouette Desire® novels and my free surprise gift. After receiving them, if I don't wish to receive anymore, I can return the shipping statement marked cancel. If I don't cancel, I will receive 6 brand-new novels every month, before they're available in stores! In the U.S.A., bill me at the bargain price of $3.80 plus 25¢ shipping and handling per book and applicable sales tax, if any*. In Canada, bill me at the bargain price of $4.47 plus 25¢ shipping and handling per book and applicable taxes**. That's the complete price and a savings of at least 10% off the cover prices—what a great deal! I understand that accepting the 2 free books and gift places me under no obligation ever to buy any books. I can always return a shipment and cancel at any time. Even if I never buy another book from Silhouette, the 2 free books and gift are mine to keep forever.

225 SDN DZ9F
326 SDN DZ9G

Name	(PLEASE PRINT)	
Address	Apt.#	
City	State/Prov.	Zip/Postal Code

Not valid to current Silhouette Desire® subscribers.

Want to try two free books from another series?
Call 1-800-873-8635 or visit www.morefreebooks.com.

* Terms and prices subject to change without notice. Sales tax applicable in N.Y.
** Canadian residents will be charged applicable provincial taxes and GST.
  All orders subject to approval. Offer limited to one per household.
® are registered trademarks owned and used by the trademark owner and or its licensee.

DES04R   ©2004 Harlequin Enterprises Limited

THE F⬢RTUNES OF TEXAS: *Reunion*

Coming in October...

The Good Doctor

by *USA TODAY* bestselling author

KAREN ROSE SMITH

Peter Clark would never describe himself as a jaw-dropping catch, despite being one of San Antonio's most respected neurosurgeons. So why is beautiful New York neurologist Violet Fortune looking at him as if she would like to show him her bedside manner?

Silhouette®

Where love comes alive™

Visit Silhouette Books at www.eHarlequin.com   FOTRTGD

Coming in November
from Silhouette Desire

DYNASTIES: THE ASHTONS

*A family built on lies…brought together
by dark, passionate secrets*

continues with

SAVOR THE SEDUCTION

by Laura Wright

Grant Ashton came
to Napa Valley to discover the truth
about his family…but found so much
more. Was Anna Sheridan, a woman
battling her own demons, the answer
to all Grant's desires?

*Available this November wherever
Silhouette books are sold.*

COMING NEXT MONTH

#1687 SAVOR THE SEDUCTION—Laura Wright
Dynasties: The Ashtons
Scandals had rocked his family but only one woman was able to shake him to the core.

#1688 BOSS MAN—Diana Palmer
Long, Tall Texans
This tough-as-leather attorney never looked twice at his dedicated assistant…until now!

#1689 HIGHLY COMPROMISED POSITION—Sara Orwig
Texas Cattleman's Club: The Secret Diary
How could she have known the sexy stranger who fathered her child was her family's sworn enemy?

#1690 THE CHASE IS ON—Brenda Jackson
The Westmorelands
His lovely new neighbor was a sweet temptation this confirmed bachelor couldn't resist.

#1691 THE RUTHLESS GROOM—Bronwyn Jameson
Princes of the Outback
She delivered the news that his bride-to-be had run away…never expecting to be next on his "to wed" list.

#1692 MISTLETOE MANEUVERS—Margaret Alison
Mixing business with pleasure could only lead to a hostile takeover…and a whole lot of passion.

SDCNM1005